West
of Devil's
Canyon

Center Point
Large Print

**This Large Print Book carries the
Seal of Approval of N.A.V.H.**

West of Devil's Canyon

RICHARD POOLE

BRISTOL PUBLIC LIBRARY
1855 Greenville Rd.
Bristolville, OH 44402
(330) 889-3651

CENTER POINT LARGE PRINT
THORNDIKE, MAINE

This Center Point Large Print edition is published
in the year 2014 by arrangement with
Golden West Literary Agency.

Copyright © 1958 by Lee E. Wells.
Copyright © renewed 1986 by the Estate of Lee E. Wells.

All rights reserved.

The text of this Large Print edition is unabridged.
In other aspects, this book may vary
from the original edition.
Printed in the United States of America
on permanent paper.
Set in 16-point Times New Roman type.

ISBN: 978-1-62899-115-4

Library of Congress Cataloging-in-Publication Data

Poole, Richard, 1907–1982.
West of Devil's Canyon / Richard Poole. —
    Center Point Large Print Edition.
    pages cm
    Summary: "Phil Ward has won the bids to provide the grading and beef
for the railroad construction west of Devil's Canyon. Now he has to not
only deal with expected hardships like weather and terrain, but also
with bushwhackers, saboteurs, and betrayal. To fail is to lose
everything, including his life"—Provided by publisher.
    ISBN 978-1-62899-115-4 (library binding : alk. paper)
    I. Title.
    PS3545.E5425W47 2014
    813'.54—dc23
                                                              2014008479

West of Devil's Canyon

I

The morning sun sent long shafts of brilliant light into the cramped hotel room, changing the brass bedstead into gleaming gold, a patina as false as rice powder on a dancehall girl. A breeze from the high mesas moved the tattered curtains at the window, over the man who stirred beneath thin blankets on the lumpy bed.

Suddenly Phil Ward's gray eyes looked blankly at the faded flowers in the wallpaper. His black hair stirred slightly as the breeze moved over the bed. He frowned momentarily, wondering where he was. Then he remembered the hotel and the little town of Latigo, near the New Mexico border. He swung his long legs to the floor, shivering slightly as the breeze touched broad shoulders and full, deep chest. Muscles rippled under the smooth skin as he reached for trousers and boots.

He stood up, a man a shade over six feet. He stepped to the window and looked down on tar-paper shacks, adobe houses and falsefront stores. A buckboard rattled in the dusty street below and a puncher swayed sleepily to the slow pace of the buckskin that carried him out to the range beyond the town.

Phil's eyes lifted to the immense plain sweeping

down from the high mesas to the north. For a second he thought he saw a tiny smudge of smoke above its far rim. Then he smiled, the easy move of the long, crooked lips softening the harsh plane of the lean cheeks, smoothing the craggy angularity of chin and jaw. The nearest Western Pacific steel was still miles beyond. But before long a glittering line of rails would bisect the plain and sweep into Latigo.

His eyes moved slowly westward until the edge of the window cut his vision. He pictured the onward reach of the rails across this high Arizona country, over the great gash of Devil's Canyon, and then through the forests about Ensign and on to the Colorado River.

He might have a part in it—an important part. The meeting today would decide. He laughed, the sound rich and throaty as he turned to the wash-stand. Two bids—one for the construction, one for furnishing beef from his Flying W to the railroad crews. Surely he'd get one; maybe even both.

Soon he slipped a black string tie under the collar of a white shirt. He lifted gunbelt and holster from the chair and strapped it about his lean hips, then slipped into a long black coat. A heavy knock interrupted him. He crossed the room in lithe strides, threw open the door. Hal Agren grinned at him, a flash of strong, white teeth. "Morning, Phil. Set for the big day?"

"Not quite. I'm hungry. Come in a minute."

Agren sat down on the edge of the bed while Phil made last minute touches on his clothes. Agren was a big man with an air as wide and breezy as the land beyond the narrow window. He wore a wide-brimmed Stetson, a black coat over a white vest that sported little spots of gold. His shirt was gleaming white and he wore a wide dark-blue cravat in which a pearl made a teardrop of light. As he sat down, the flair of his coat revealed a handsomely tooled gunbelt.

He took off his hat and placed it on the bed. He ran long fingers carefully along his temple, smoothing his gold hair. His blue eyes were bright and eager and mobile lips over a cleft chin sobered for an instant. "A hell of a big day for us, Phil."

"Getting nervous?" Phil asked.

Agren laughed, throwing back his head. "Not on your life, Mr. Ward!"

Phil brushed his hair, catching Agren's reflection in the wavy mirror. He had a brash confidence, a friendly heartiness that would instantly put anyone off guard. Not that guard was needed with Hal Agren, Phil thought. He was too open, too pleasantly boastful, too sure of success and glad to tell you all about it.

Both men came from Ensign, but until they had chanced to meet on the road and learned that each headed for Latigo, they had never met. Now Phil wondered idly how that had happened. A man like Hal Agren would be hard to miss in so small a town as Ensign. However, building up his Flying W had kept Phil close to the ranch these last few years. That, and the fact that Agren was a new arrival, might explain it.

Phil picked up his black hat and adjusted the broad brim, and turned to grin at Hal. "Let's face the day."

They walked the short distance to the town's single cafe. They soon attacked the platters of eggs and ham, the reviving, pleasant bite of strong coffee. Phil glanced at the big clock on the back wall, thinking that the hands moved much too slowly.

Agren pushed aside his plate and signaled the waitress to bring more coffee. "Well, Phil, by tonight we'll be in business for the railroad—contractors."

Phil smiled, then sobered. "Funny thing, Hal. I'm sure my bids are right. Yet now I'm scared. It's a hell of a job building railroad from Devil's Canyon west to the Colorado!"

Hal chuckled. "I'm not worried. Rail ties—Lord, I've got enough standing timber to cover all of Arizona with 'em!" He rubbed his hands together in satisfaction. "My luck sure holds!" He caught Phil's puzzled look. "I bought that land three years ago, sight unseen, figuring I could hold it a while and sell at a fair profit. I fooled around Tucson for a year and then, came to Ensign to see what I'd bought. About that time Western

Pacific announced it was building through and I knew they'd need lumber. So—here I am. That timber will make me a fortune!"

"If you get the contract," Phil warned, "and if everything goes right after you get it."

"I'll get it, and so will you." Hal twisted about to look at the clock. "I'm getting nervous. Let's see what Latigo looks like."

They walked slowly along the single main street that had two saloons, a stable, false-front stores and a small church with a stubby, white steeple. This was Latigo, and the only thing that gave it importance was the meeting—an hour away—the Western Pacific had called for awarding bids.

Phil and Hal strolled along until they came to one of the saloons. Two saddled horses stood at the hitchrack, heads hanging low as though they had just finished a long and tiring journey.

Phil's eyes rested idly on the brands. He stopped short. "Lazy R! That's Milt Reiger's spread. What's he doing in Latigo!"

Agren frowned. "Reiger? From Ensign?"

"Yes, damn him," Phil snapped. "He has a hardcase crew run by a gunswift segundo, Dave Trego. Reiger's not much better himself."

"Outlaw?"

"Not around Ensign. But I've heard he was a ridge runner in the Big Bend country. No proof."

Agren made a restless motion. "Phil, there's still some time to waste. Let's have a drink. I need one."

11

Phil laughed, "Nerves, Hal? I guess I need one, too."

They walked a few yards to the second of the town's saloons. The place, like the town, was a copy of a myriad others. A man behind the bar spoke cheerfully, mentioned the weather and then left them alone with their drinks.

Hal picked up his glass and turned to Phil. "To us and the railroad—may all of us thrive."

Phil drank the toast and Agren immediately ordered another. The batwings whispered and footsteps sounded loud in the almost empty room, the clink of the spurs musical. They stopped abruptly and a heavy voice broke the silence.

"Hell, all of Ensign's here!"

The bar mirror reflected Milt Reiger and Dave Trego. Phil slowly turned. "Howdy, Milt . . . Dave."

Milt's bullet head hunched between his shoulders. He veered toward the far end of the bar and growled an order. Dave Trego gave Phil a thin smile and joined Reiger.

An uneasy silence descended. Phil had no idea what had brought Reiger to Latigo but he didn't like it. Reiger's spread bordered his own, and often Lazy R riders had strayed far into Phil's range. They had apparently done nothing but wander far and wide, yet Phil had been uneasy.

Reiger hooked his elbow on the bar, pushed his shapeless hat back on short, wiry black hair that thinned just above the low forehead. His smile, intended to be friendly, was hardly more than a grimace of thick lips. "Surprised to see you, Ward. You here for the biddings?"

It was Phil's turn to be surprised. He nodded. "You?"

"Sure, and I'll get it, too. I can skin any rancher in these parts on price."

Phil shrugged. "Then I'll be sorry when they give the bids."

"You ain't trying for the beef contract!" Reiger demanded. He nudged Trego.

Trego glanced at Phil with mottled green eyes. Dave Trego was an enigma. He was tall, and so thin that every wind must blow right through him. He was all knobby elbows and knees, a scarecrow whose nondescript clothes hung baggily from a bony frame.

His neck was long, with an Adam's apple that bobbled convulsively as he swallowed his drink. His head was narrow, the high forehead sloping, the skin yellow and pulled tightly across the bones.

"Man, you ain't got a chance!" Reiger crowed.

Trego spoke in a throaty voice, lips barely moving in his skull-like face. "Don't brand your dogies until you've roped 'em, Milt."

Reiger laughed. "Why, Dave, you know how we stand!"

He turned again to the bar. Agren finished his drink and Phil's head moved imperceptibly toward the door. Agren nodded and they walked to the batwings. Some impulse made Phil look back. Reiger watched him, still grinning. But it was Trego who held Phil's attention. There was cold calculation in the green eyes, as though he considered how swiftly Phil could reach the gun holstered under his coat. It was a startling thing that sent a tingle along the nape of Phil's neck.

He pushed through the batwings, feeling it must have been a trick of the dim light. Yet there was something deadly about Trego. Phil shrugged it off; there was no reason he and Trego should clash.

It seemed the next two hours would never pass. They sat on the hotel porch and watched the thin traffic of Latigo. Other men came out, spoke with distant politeness and took the remaining chairs. Reiger and Trego appeared in the doorway of the saloon. Phil watched Reiger hitch his gunbelt on his big paunch and then cross the street with a confident stride. Trego followed like a hungry ghost. They joined the group on the porch, Reiger giving all of them a contemptuous, sweeping glance. Trego closed his eyes and leaned against the wall.

A thin man with spectacles that rode the ridge of a long nose appeared in the doorway. He looked about the group. "Gentlemen, Mr. Fleming is about to announce the bids for Western Pacific. He is waiting."

A clatter arose as the men came to sudden life. Chairs scraped and boots thudded across the floor of the porch. Reiger swung around, elbowed the first man out of the way, and led the procession into the hotel. . . .

Western Pacific had taken over the dining room. Chairs had been neatly arranged in rows before a long table where a man sat, a bundle of papers in his hand. Phil and Agren found seats. There was a period of rustling, a quick lift of talk that swiftly died. Attention centered on the man behind the table. He was not tall, but he gave the impression of tremendous vitality. His face was square and rugged, softened by the innate laughter of the lips, the alert and understanding gleam of the brown eyes set deep under craggy brows.

He had dignity, leavened by a human warmth, apparent even in these first few moments. It showed in the patience with which he waited for the men to get settled and comfortable. It was apparent in the quick, yet reserved smile he gave all of them.

The balding clerk took his place at the far end of the table, fussily arranged papers, opened a bottle of ink, dipped his pen, and held it poised. There was silence.

The chief engineer broke the tension. "Gentlemen, I am Rayburn Fleming. Each of you has made a bid covering various work and materials in the building of the Western Pacific Railroad west from Devil's Canyon to the Colorado River. These bids have been carefully considered, not only as to price but also as to your record for past performance and character. The railroad has to consider ability to fulfill a contract as well as the amount bid. This is to help you understand why your bid was—or was not—accepted."

His sharp eyes swept about the room. He smiled gravely. "Your contracts," he touched a stack of papers, "contain penalty clauses to be invoked if the quality and quantity of materials is not right, or if the speed of your work is not satisfactory."

Reiger stirred. "Sure. Get on with it."

Fleming's eyes flashed and his jaw set. Then he turned to the clerk and nodded. There was a nervous shuffling, then a tense silence. Fleming opened the first document, the crackling of the paper loud in the room. In a clear, precise voice he read the figures of the successful bid, the name of the bidder.

The contracts covered all phases of railroad building, from the main jobs to secondary ones, small but important. As he read each contract, some man would smile jubilantly while others would frown and bite their lips. There was constant movement as the losers quietly arose and left the room.

"To furnish rail ties of specified quality and quantities," Fleming's deep voice rolled on. Hal Agren's knuckles whitened on his hatbrim. As

Fleming read the prices, a look of hope came in Agren's eyes and his breath expelled in a loud sigh when Fleming said, "Awarded to Mr. Hal Agren of Ensign, Arizona Territory."

Agren turned to Phil with a swift, flashing smile and his gesture was wide. "I knew it!" he exclaimed.

Fleming came to the grading contract and Phil's breath caught. Then his name was read and, like the rest, his breath eased out in a relieved sigh. The voice went on.

"For furnishing beef of specified number and quality to the railroad construction crews, and crews of the subcontractors," Fleming intoned. Reiger hunched forward, as did Phil. "Mr. Phil Ward of the Flying W, Ensign, Arizona Territory."

Both contracts! Phil sat dazed. Agren pounded his back in congratulation. "Man! You've done it! There's nothing like our luck. Ride with me, boy, and we'll build this railroad ourselves!"

Fleming looked up and his teeth flashed in a warm, understanding smile. "Hardly that, sir, but both of you will certainly help."

Reiger suddenly came to his feet, his chair crashing back. His ugly face tightened and his brows knotted. Trego tried to check him but Reiger's bull voice already filled the room. "I bid on that beef. My price was way below Ward's."

Fleming looked at him. "You are . . ."

"Milt Reiger—Lazy R."

Fleming shrugged. "I explained, Mr. Reiger, how Western Pacific selected the winning bids."

Reiger's fist clenched. "You saying I ain't to be trusted, mister?"

Fleming's eyes flashed. He arose, and Phil saw that he did not wear a gun. "I did not choose the bids, Mr. Reiger. I merely know that Mr. Ward was given the contract."

Reiger's heavy face flushed and his right hand dropped to his side, near the holstered gun. Phil eased to his feet. Trego caught the movement but he gave his attention to Reiger.

Reiger's head was hunched now, eyes dangerous. "I know why. It's plain as pony tracks. He paid off, that's why! Maybe you got some of it, Fleming."

Fleming jerked as though he had been struck. His neck and cheeks turned red and his fists clenched. He circled the table, his jaw hard. Men pushed away, and the clerk's face turned paper-white. Phil moved between the engineer and Reiger.

Fleming's strong arm barred Phil as his eyes locked with Reiger's. "I resent that, sir!"

"Resent and be damned," Reiger bellowed, as his hand lifted to his gun. "I know a crooked deal when I smell one—and this is it."

Phil swept aside the skirt of his coat and his own hand moved toward the holstered Colt. Trego caught the movement. His eyes flashed a deadly warning and then he cut between Reiger and Fleming.

"Milt," he said, his voice flat, but dominating. "This ain't the time." Reiger tried to push him aside but Trego held his ground. "Milt, clear out and shut up."

Reiger glared at him, but read something in Trego's steady, mottled eyes. Reiger took a deep breath. He glared over Trego's shoulders at Fleming and then at Phil.

The fingers of the hand hovering over the gun opened and closed and then the arm dropped. He spoke in a choked voice. "I know when I been cheated, and I ain't one to take it. Fleming, you'll sure as hell hear from me again. That goes double for you, Ward. You can make your tally on it."

He turned on his heel and strode from the room. Trego looked at the engineer and Phil. The death's-head face was expressionless but the green eyes were alight, pleased. His voice was soft. "He means it, gents."

Fleming and Phil watched them go. Agren stood behind Phil, fair face drawn, eyes rounded. Phil turned to Fleming. "Sorry it happened. But Trego's telling the truth. Reiger won't forget."

"And I don't frighten, Mr. Ward," Fleming snapped. His voice grew sharp. "Do you?"

Phil shook his head. "It takes a lot to scare me, Fleming."

II

Late in the afternoon Phil stretched out on the bed, studying the ceiling. He must be sure that each head of beef reached the railroad, that each mile of track was graded on time to pass inspection. The contract penalties could easily wipe him out. His Flying W had plenty of beef and he had figured the construction at a conservative figure. But there was still the unexpected. He would have to guard against that.

He had sent a telegram to Tim Moriarty in Cheyenne, confirming the big Irishman's employment as superintendent and asking him to come immediately to Ensign. There were a million things to be done and a very short time in which to do them. Western Pacific built swiftly westward, making track-laying records each day.

There was a knock at the door and Hal Agren came in. He carried a bottle and a glass, grinned at Phil and placed them on the washstand. He poured drinks and handed one to Phil. "It's time you and me celebrated."

Phil laughed and accepted the drink. "I guess we should, at that. Here's hoping." Phil lifted his glass.

Agren drank and then sobered. "I thought we'd

have real trouble today when Reiger acted up. He looked ready for gunplay."

"I don't think he'd have gone that far," Phil said. "Anyhow, Trego stopped him."

"Trego," Agren repeated with a slight shudder. "He looks like walking death. Who is he?"

"Simon-pure gunhawk. If you can believe the stories, he has notches all over his gun. He likes killing."

A knock again sounded on the door and Phil, puzzled, opened it. The balding clerk peered through his spectacles. "Mr. Fleming would like to see you." He saw Hal Agren. "Oh, and you, too, Mr. Agren. Right away, in his room. . . ."

Fleming greeted them, offered drinks that Phil refused and Agren accepted. The engineer spoke pleasantly about generalities for a time, then came to the point. "You'll be leaving soon for Ensign, gentlemen?"

"In the morning," Phil answered.

Fleming nodded. "Good. Both of you are new in this construction game and I'd like to see you make a solid profit. I can't stress too much that speed is of the essence. We're building closer every day and, before long, our crew will be starting the trestle over Devil's Canyon."

"So far ahead?" Agren asked, surprised.

"We want the trestle finished by the time the rails have reached the canyon, so there'll be no delay. Once we're across, your work begins."

"We'll be ready," Agren spoke up quickly.

"I'm sure of it," Fleming said. "In any case, I'll be in Ensign to set up general construction offices. If I can help in any way, I'll be at your service."

"Thanks, but I don't think I'll need it," Agren said.

Phil smiled. "I'd appreciate that, Mr. Fleming. Things can always happen."

"That they can," Fleming nodded. "I've been building railroads all my life. This is a rough, fast game. It never goes smoothly." Agren flushed slightly, but Fleming continued speaking to Phil. "Both grading and beef, Mr. Ward. A strange combination of contracts. Can you handle them?"

"My Flying W spread is one of the best in northern Arizona. My segundo and crew can run the ranch and meet the beef quota. I've hired a construction superintendent who knows his business."

"Who is the man?"

"Tim Moriarty."

Fleming's face lighted. "Good! Big Tim! He likes to build railroads, fight and eat—in that order. That gives you an edge, Mr. Ward. And you, Mr. Agren?"

"Why, nothing to worry on my part. I've got the timber, and the crews. We'll build camps right away and put in skid roads. Sawmill equipment will be in Ensign within a month. I'll be cutting and treating ties long before you hit Devil's Canyon."

Fleming nodded again. "We'll have little trouble then. I must again warn you about those penalty clauses, Mr. Agren. If you fail, you *could* end up badly in debt. Mr. Ward, yours are doubled because of the two contracts. Take every precaution to deliver. We want to make damn sure our schedule will be maintained."

"I'll do my best, naturally."

"That's it then, gentlemen." Fleming held out his hand to Phil then to Agren. "I'll see you in Ensign before very long. I look forward to it."

By morning Phil was as eager as Agren to get back home and start things moving. They had agreed they would make the long ride to Ensign together. It was a journey of several days and Phil came to know Hal Agren better. At first the man's breezi-ness and almost cocky confidence annoyed him, but he detected a shrewd brain behind the open, half-braggart air. Nor did Hal shirk any of his share of camp duties. He was filled with ideas, and Phil came to know that this railroad contract was a stepping stone to even greater things for Hal Agren. Phil would listen as they sat before the fire, pulling at his pipe, nodding now and then.

Once Hal broke off sharply and squinted across the flames at him. "I've been talking about me. What about you, Phil? Figure on setting the world on fire?"

Phil chuckled. "Maybe, if I happen to have the match. But I won't worry about it. If the bank account's comfortable and I'm happy, I can't see any point in using Spanish spurs on my own flanks."

Agren grimaced. "That sounds peaceful, but it's not for me."

Phil nodded. "I guess it depends on how much we want."

"Why, man, you can't begin to name it! Money, more land than you can ride over in a week, everything that goes with it! And you can add the most beautiful woman in the world for my wife."

"Who is she?" Phil asked, surprised.

Agren laughed. "I haven't found her yet. But when I do, I'll get her and no one will stop me."

"Even the girl?" Phil asked.

"She won't have a chance. I'll sweep her off her feet." Agren sobered. "How about you, Phil? Have you got room for a wife in your plans?"

"Some time. Like you, I think I'll know her when she comes along." Phil laughed, arose and stretched. "Let's hit the blankets."

Their road led far to the south to avoid the great gash of Devil's Canyon and then angled north and west again, a huge detour that the railroad would eventually eliminate. The road followed one lip of the gorge, the far bank tantalizingly out of reach. It made an irritating and troublesome journey, but this time Phil didn't mind. He now worked to bridge that gap and, besides, Agren's constant cheerfulness, his gay whistle, his wide boastfulness helped speed the hours and the miles.

At last they were on the western side and the way to Ensign lay clear before them. That night they made another camp and, after the evening meal, sprawled before the fire. They had spent the time in lazy talk and now Agren poked thoughtfully at the embers.

"Phil, I've been thinking about your beef. Will the railroad take all of it?"

"No, there'll be some to spare."

Agren nodded. "Maybe you and I can do business. I got lumber camps to feed. It's not a long drive from your ranch. You could supply the beef. If you're good enough for Western Pacific, you're good enough for Hal Agren!"

They discussed the details and within a short time had come to an agreement. Hal was elated to solve this problem and Phil pleased to find another market so close at hand. They shook hands on it.

"Something else, Hal. Both of us have a big job to do, and we have to work mighty close. We should be ready to help one another if things go wrong."

"Team up?" Hal asked shortly.

Phil shook his head. "No, remain independent. But you'll need my beef to keep rolling, and I'll need your rail ties. We could work together to make sure both of us make the grade."

Agren pursed his lips and studied Phil a moment, then smiled. "It makes sense. Let's work it that way."

Again they shook hands and Phil settled back in his blanket. Agren yawned and stretched. His arms were still high in the air when the gun roared and flashed from the outer darkness and the bullet whipped across the fire, ripping through Phil's shirt sleeve.

Phil moved without conscious thought. He dropped, rolled toward the protection of the night. Another bullet kicked up dirt where he had been a split second before and he realized there must be two men out there.

Agren remained frozen for a second, and then a slug kicked up embers and sparks at his feet. He jerked away and threw himself toward the edge of the firelight.

Phil rolled into darkness, and pulled his gun. He threw himself around and saw the flash of gunfire and threw a swift shot at the flash. Instantly another gun from a different direction spat flame and the bullet whined over his head. Phil slammed a couple of bullets toward the second ambusher and then plunged away again.

Now Agren's gun joined in the battle. Phil held his Colt poised, hammer dogged back, ready to line and fire at the answering gun flashes. But they didn't come. The black night remained unbroken. He heard the horses stomp and pull at the pickets, but there was no other sound.

"Phil!" Hal called.

Instantly a gun sought him out, the unseen ambusher firing toward the voice. Phil, jaw set, threw a bullet toward the flame, the only target he had. He heard a curse, a threshing and then silence. He waited, tense, not wanting to fire blindly and attract more searching lead. Agren now made no sound, having learned his lesson.

Time dragged. Phil tried to probe into the concealing darkness and his ears strained for the slightest noise. Once he heard a stir off to his left and his head instantly swiveled in that direction, but the noise was not repeated. The fire still flickered and glowed and he could see his crumpled blankets.

He considered easing around the fire, cutting off to his right. He might find the bushwhackers and at least have a chance to fight. But they might be waiting for just such a move.

The sound to his left was repeated again, much closer. He whipped about, gun leveled, straining to hear. He could make out only faint, unmoving shadows.

"Phil?" The voice made a soft sound nearby.

"Hal!" He replied softly, relieved. "I thought you were one of them. Keep quiet."

"Who are they?"

Phil hissed him to silence and probed the night again. Even the horses were quiet now. Phil bit at his lip, checking over the probable next move of the ambushers. "Hal," he whispered at last, "stay where you are. I'm going to make a circle. If I flush them, come shooting."

There was a moment's silence. "Sure, Phil. I'll . . . back you."

Phil moved soundlessly off into the darkness. He advanced a few feet at a time and then stopped to listen. Once his hand encountered a stone and his fingers wrapped around it. He smiled grimly, and threw it with all his power far into the night. In a few seconds it landed with a dull thud some distance away and Phil lifted his Colt.

He heard a stir behind him and knew Agren had been alarmed by the sound. But there was nothing else, no sudden spurt of gunfire. The silence lengthened and Phil stood frowning, tense. He finally knew that the bushwhackers were gone—felt the certainty of it.

But he did not abandon caution. It took him some time to work in a huge circle about the fire and drift up to their picketed horses. They stood quietly, merely pricking their ears at his approach.

Phil felt the emptiness of the night. He moved several yards from the horses and crouched, below the probable line of a bullet. Then he called Hal, ducked even lower. Agren's cautious voice answered from a distance. Phil looked about and slowly rose. "Circle the fire, Hal. I'll wait for you."

He did not want to get careless at the last moment and make a clean target of himself or Agren before the fire. The bushwhackers might have pulled back a distance, waiting for the two men to show themselves.

Evidently Agren had the same idea, for it seemed an interminable time before Phil heard a stir and Agren's bulky shadow appeared beside him. His voice was low. "No sign of 'em, Phil?"

"Nothing yet. We'll scout about, but I think they're gone."

They were. A quarter-hour of careful scouting failed to give them any trace of the bush-whackers. Only then did their tension leave them. They returned to the fire, and Phil instantly kicked it out.

"In case they come back," he said to Agren. "Sleep with your hand close to your gun."

"Who were they?" Agren asked shakily.

"Probably outlaws on the run and they happened to see us," Phil said. "A couple who wanted some good horses and our money."

"It was close!" Agren breathed. "Too close!"

Phil moved far away from the dead campfire, suggesting Agren do the same. If the prowlers returned, they would walk into a trap. Phil rolled up in his blankets but it was a long time before he drifted off. He heard too many night noises and knew that his nerves were still on edge.

The next morning they again circled the camp, looking for signs. Phil soon found it, the bright gleam of brass shells. He called Agren over and they looked further, Agren obviously unused to searching for trail. In a few moments Phil called him again.

"They tethered their animals here," he said, and turned to look toward the distant camp. "They probably saw our fire and decided to look us over."

"But where did they come from?" Agren asked blankly. "Where did they go?"

Phil followed the faint trace of the trail with his eyes and it led him back toward Devil's Canyon. He spoke slowly, "I think they followed us, Hal. Looks that way. Let's take another pasear."

He soon discovered that the trail led north and west. There would be no point in following, for the bushwhackers had ridden fast. They already had many hours' start, and Phil was certain that within a mile or two the sign would vanish. He turned back to the camp, Agren with him, puzzled.

"They headed toward Ensign, Hal," Phil said soberly, "and they trailed us here."

"From Latigo?"

"Might be." Phil frowned. "There's no proof, but Milt Reiger did a lot of threatening back there. And there were two of them who jumped us last night."

Agren stared at Phil. "Reiger and Trego! Sure?"

"No, but I'd gamble on it. I figured Reiger was just blowing off mad, but this looks as if he means it. You and I will have to keep our eyes open, Hal."

"But he threatened you!" Agren protested.

"And shot at us both last night," Phil added dryly. "I guess they think we're partners. From now on I watch your back and you watch mine."

"Sure," Agren said, looking troubled. "Sure!"

Phil missed the thin edge of uncertainty in his tone.

III

Late the next afternoon, they arrived in Ensign. There had been no further sign of the ambushers and Agren's mercurial spirits arose to their usual heights. He seemed to have completely forgotten the swift, deadly incident.

For some time now they had been riding through forest broken here and there with great stretches of rich grass. But gradually the trees closed in and finally conquered. Only to the north of Ensign would the grass again come into its own, high and rich. It was here that Phil's Flying W beef grazed and grew fat. Just beyond, Milt Reiger's Lazy R stretched back into the lifting benchlands of the mountains. Agren's holdings spread through this forest country, bounding Flying W to the south and west, half circling Ensign.

The road twisted through the trees and Ensign lay before them, a spread of buildings pleasantly shaded by pine and fir. Low log houses faced the street and gradually gave way to a double row of false-front, frame stores. Phil and Agren moved toward the heart of town. On the planked sidewalks of the short business district there was an air of bustle and business that had increased even in the short time they had been away.

Phil pulled aside before Jim Loman's big store.

"I start work here, Hal. We'll get together on the details of that beef deal."

"Make it soon. My first camp will be in operation before you know it." Agren sobered. "Take care of yourself. If you were right about those two, this is their stomping ground."

"And mine. I'll watch, and the same to you."

Agren moved on down the street. Phil tethered the horse and crossed the plank sidewalk. The big main room of the store was crowded and Phil worked his way down the long aisle, around the potbellied stove in the rear and knocked on a door, then pushed it open. Jim Loman wheeled ponderously around from the roll-top desk and peered at him over the top of his spectacles.

"Howdy, Phil. Congratulations!" The fat man chuckled at Phil's puzzled look. "Reiger was in early this morning. I hear you cheated him, bought off the whole Western Pacific. Don't know how you'll make any money that way, but Reiger swears that's how it happened."

Phil grimaced and sat down in a straight-back chair near the desk. Jim Loman, a mountain of a man, folded dimpled hands over his paunch and his brown eyes twinkled. "I guess you and me will do a lot of business."

"Lots of it, Jim. Get off that order for picks, shovels, scrapers and graders. Right away."

"Figured you'd say that, Phil. Sent the order off right after Reiger called you a son of a bitch.

Ought to be well toward Devil's Canyon by now."

"When can we expert shipment?"

"Month—maybe. I'll keep pushing 'em. Anything else you want?"

"Later, and plenty. Everything it takes to build a construction camp Can you handle it?"

"Sure, Phil. Just give me advance warning."

Phil arose, feeling the elephantine man's warmth and friendliness. As he left the office, it occurred to him that he'd better see to the building of an office shack in town. He headed for the lumber yard.

The weeks that followed were busy, with a thousand details to be watched and checked, a hundred unexpected tasks that no one could foresee. He was constantly between his ranch and the town, and he had no chance even to talk to Agren until the day he waited for the stage that would bring Tim Moriarty. That day Phil was waiting patiently on the hotel porch when Agren came out of the lobby and stopped short, his face lighting.

"Man! Haven't seen hide or hair of you! Where you been?"

"Too busy to breathe, Hal." Phil briefly summarized the weeks and Agren listened sympathetically. "How about you?"

"Just as busy," Agren said with a laugh. "Building lumber camps and hiring men. They're about ready to cut right now! I've got the saw-mill up and I'm waiting for the equipment. Say, your stuff and mine will come by the same shipment! Just checked with Loman."

"It's on its way?" Phil asked quickly.

"Rail to Albuquerque and freight wagon around Devil's Canyon."

The stage appeared at the far end of the street and soon drew up before the hotel. Agren had hurried away and Phil stepped down on the walk. Three passengers descended and then a fourth man backed out, straightened and turned. He was immense. Phil wondered how the others had managed to squeeze in beside him. He towered over six feet, had beam shoulders, a barrel chest, and legs like tree trunks. His clothing strained at every seam in its effort to cover the great, muscular body. His face was square, the nose broad and upturned, the skin freckled. Blue eyes twinkled from beneath shaggy red brows.

He saw Phil, and easily pushed through the crowd. "Ye'd be Phil Ward? I'm Tim Moriarty."

Phil accepted the huge hand, wincing at tortured fingers. Tim shoved his hat back on a freckled forehead, revealing hair as red as a grass fire.

Phil flexed his numb fingers behind his back. "It's been a long trip, Tim, and you'll want to rest."

Tim's lifted hand checked him. "Have ye a place for me to work, bucko?"

"Of course. Right down the street."

"Then we'll have a drink to cut the dust from me throat. We'll have another to our meeting and a third to be sociable. Then, if ye please, I'll start on me work."

"But—"

"*Whsst,* and would ye listen to an old railroad builder, lad! There is much to be done. We'll have the time now and then to be sociable and 'tis many a bottle we'll empty, I promise. Now—where do I work?"

Within an hour Tim had had his drinks, studied the grading contracts, and had the survey maps of the railroad spread out before him. He waved Phil away. "Come back tomorrow, bucko. By then I'll know how much dirt is to be moved and what we'll need in men and equipment."

Phil left the new shack with the feeling that a genie had taken a load from his back, and following days proved him right. Tim hired men and began to build the construction camp just west of Devil's Canyon. Phil felt he could forget those problems. . . .

Letters came to both Phil and Agren from Fleming. He would be in Ensign in two weeks to set up permanent headquarters for the railroad. Phil had just finished reading his letter and had tossed it to Tim when Agren came in, holding his letter aloft.

"Fleming's coming!"

"I know." Phil indicated the paper in Tim's

huge hands and introduced Agren. Hal looked in mild amazement at the big Irishman.

"He's big enough to be the whole work gang!"

Tim's booming laugh broke out. " 'Tis a deception of the eyes, Mr. Agren. It would take five thousand of the likes of me to build a railroad." He sobered and indicated the letter. "I know Rayburn Fleming, and he's a man that likes to see things done."

"Let him." Agren grinned and dropped into a seat. "I'll have a few things to show him."

Tim's blue eyes threw Agren a swift glance. "Will ye now! I'll get ye me wages 'twill not satisfy Rayburn."

Agren passed it off, turning to Phil to describe his progress in detail. Now and then Tim lifted a shaggy brow, moved his lips wryly, but said nothing. Finally Agren arose and offered to buy them drinks, which they refused. With a last airy word he left.

Tim stared at the closed door. "Now there is a lad," he said slowly, "who works a deal with his mouth and with little else."

"You wrong him, Tim," Phil said.

"That may be, but have ye noticed the way he blows it up when he talks? It would not be wise to put a test to the lad."

"The railroad will. He furnishes the ties."

"That it will, and we shall see what kind of man he is."

● ● ●

Again some two weeks later, Phil waited for the stage. He sat in one of the chairs on the hotel porch and frowned out at the busy street. It was filled with wagons and riders, a constantly changing picture. One of the riders veered toward the hotel, and, with a start, Phil looked into Milt Reiger's heavy, scowling face. Just behind him, Trego worked his way through a press and then urged his horse forward.

Reiger looked for trouble. It was clear in the hunch of the beefy shoulders, the way the dark brows pulled down. Phil's jaw set. Just then Trego worked his horse over toward Reiger and spoke fast. There was a brief flash of anger in the cadaverous face. Then Reiger veered off and the two continued down the street. Just before they were swallowed in the traffic, Reiger looked back and, even at this distance, Phil felt the impact of his hatred. Then they were gone.

Phil whirled about when a hand fell on his shoulder, then smiled apologetically as Agren stared at him in surprise. Phil pointed up the street. "Milt Reiger just passed and I thought he was going to speak."

Agren's eyes widened, then he grinned. "He didn't? Then I wouldn't let it bother me. I'd almost forgotten about him."

"So had I," Phil said, "and that could be a mistake."

Agren sat down in the next chair. He was dressed immaculately in dark trousers and coat, cravat and white vest. He was eager and peered constantly down the street. Phil suddenly thought of what Tim had said. He couldn't quite agree. Agren was ambitious and a bit boastful, but he seemed to be able to back it. Who could argue with that?

The stage rocked up the street to the hotel. Phil and Agren both arose when it came to a dust-raising halt before the hotel. The driver jumped down and opened the door. Fleming descended, and turned to assist someone else from the coach.

Phil had an impression of cornsilk hair under a pert bonnet, and full, sultry lips. Blue-gray eyes met his for a second and eagerly moved on. His breath caught. She was so unexpected, so beautiful. Agren openly stared, lips parted.

Fleming saw them. "Ward! Agren! I didn't expect you this soon!" He caught Agren's admiring stare at the girl and his gray eyes twinkled. "May I present Mr. Hal Agren and Mr. Phil Ward, Carol? My sister, gentlemen."

Agren instantly took the slender hand she extended as his eyes boldly searched her face. She turned to Phil. She was even more beautiful than he had first imagined. Her eyes were not quite on a level with his own. Her face had Fleming's squareness about the jaw and chin, but delicately softened. The nose was short, a trifle broad, but this was no defect.

She wore a gray traveling dress, the skirt long and gathered in the modified bustle of the period. The dress was high-necked, adorned by an exquisite cameo brooch at the collar. Her hair had a slightly reddish tint, a hint of her brother's color.

Phil suddenly felt awkward and tongue-tied. His face grew warm when her eyes met his directly and his voice stumbled over his words of greeting.

Her voice was clear and musical. "It's a pleasure, Mr. Ward."

Agren jostled Phil. "We hope you enjoy Ensign, Miss Fleming. I'll show you around, if I may."

"I'd like that," she nodded. She looked again at Phil. "This country is so different from that around Albuquerque."

"Yes, it is," he said inanely, wondering desperately where his wits had gone.

He covered his confusion by accepting the luggage the driver passed down from the rack atop the coach. Fleming helped him, but Agren talked easily to Carol, making the best of his first impression. At last the final carpetbag sat at Phil's feet and Fleming brushed the dust from his hands.

"Gentlemen, if you will excuse us." Agren's face fell. Fleming smiled. "We've had a long journey. As soon as we have rested, I will contact you at—say your office, Ward?"

"That will be fine," Agren cut in and looked at Carol. "Maybe dinner afterwards?"

She smiled but did not fully accept. "Perhaps."

The hotel porter had gathered up their bags, so Fleming took Carol's arm. Phil and Agren swept off their hats as she turned with her brother and disappeared through the door. They found themselves staring foolishly at the empty door.

Agren replaced his hat, looked at Phil. "Fleming's sister . . . imagine! She's a beauty!"

Phil nodded, still seeing the play of light in those eyes that were sometimes gray and sometimes blue. Agren squared his shoulders. "This, my friend, calls for another drink!"

Phil glanced toward the hotel. "Is it wise? Fleming will—"

"See us when he's ready, and that will be some time. Besides, there's good reason for a drink. It's on me. She makes me feel as though I own the whole world."

Phil laughed and stepped off the walk, but Agren checked him. His voice was serious. "Did you ever see such a girl, Phil? I'm going to take every minute of her time! I never thought about it before, but she's the kind of woman I'd like to have for my wife."

Phil jerked around in surprise. He kept his voice level. "I've had the same idea, Hal."

Agren stared, then broke into a wide grin. "You

won't have a chance. I'll see to it!" He laughed. "Let's have that drink—to her and the man who wins her."

He headed across the street to the saloon. Phil looked back at the hotel, then slowly followed. He sensed that despite the laughter something closely akin to rivalry had started between him and Hal Agren.

Agren waited on the saloon porch, and together they pushed through the batwings. Even at this time of day the place did a brisk business and the bar was almost solidly lined. However, Agren pushed a way to the rail, his wide and friendly grin soothing any chance irritation.

He ordered drinks, held his glass to Phil, repeated his toast to Carol, and downed the liquor. Phil met the toast and then glanced at the big back mirror. His eyes locked with Reiger's who stood a few feet down the bar, hidden up to now by the intervening customers.

Phil's lips flattened and he spoke hurriedly to Agren. "Reiger's here, Hal. He's been drinking. Let's leave before he has a chance to act up."

Agren nodded, turned to place his glass on the bar as Phil walked toward the door. He had taken a few steps when Reiger's harsh voice halted him in mid-stride.

"Ward! Running off?"

Phil slowly turned. Reiger stood a few feet away, spread-legged and arrogant. Trego's lean figure made a black and menacing silhouette behind him.

"Running from what, Milt?"

"From me, maybe." His murky eyes gleamed. "I see you and that damn engineer who cheated me got together again."

Phil took a deep breath. "Reiger, we argued this in Latigo. On the way back, someone tried with bullets—at night. Both arguments were lost."

Milt glared. "You're saying I tried to bushwhack you?"

"Did you?" Phil asked levelly.

Milt's eyes narrowed, skittered to the crowd, back to Phil. "You'll never tie that bushwhack to me. I'm saying right to your face there was some deal between you and that engineer."

"You're wrong, Reiger, but this isn't the time or the place to talk about it. Everything's settled and nothing can change it."

"Is it?" Reiger came slowly toward Phil and a deep hush settled over the room. Trego moved silently behind him. His bony fingers lightly brushed his holster and something in the tight set of the man's face told Phil that this time Trego would back his boss.

"Nothing's settled," Reiger said again. His head hunched forward, his right arm was held akimbo, the fingers spread a scant inch from his Colt. There was a swift movement of the crowd getting out of the probable line of fire. "You

43

don't figure to cheat me and get away with it?"

"Reiger, there was no cheating," Phil said evenly.

"Like hell! Think I don't know you slipped some extra money to Fleming!"

Reiger was determined to have a showdown. Phil could see it. He might handle the rancher alone, but Dave Trego stacked the odds against him. Phil eased onto the balls of his feet. Trego was the real danger.

"I bought nobody, Reiger. The contract was honestly awarded." Phil looked at the thin gunman. "Dave, what's the point of all this? Take him home."

"He runs the show," Trego said shortly, a slight blur in his voice showing he was also mean with whisky.

"You bet I run it," Reiger growled and his head set lower between his beefy shoulders. His voice thickened with lashing anger. "And I call the tune, Ward. I say you're a cheating, crooked bastard!"

Here it was . . . the snapping of the trap. Reiger expected gunplay and he had fallen into a half crouch, his hand slashing down for his Colt.

But Phil lunged toward him, right fist slamming into Reiger's stomach, his left taloning around the man's gun wrist, jamming the Colt deep in the holster. Reiger's breath blasted out and his fingers spasmodically opened as he doubled forward. Phil released the man's wrist, caught the gun and flipped it out of the holster. He kicked it spinning across the floor to be lost amid the feet of the crowded onlookers.

Trego was surprised by the sudden turn Phil had given the fight. Moving with desperate speed, Phil turned Reiger half around so that he blocked Trego's draw. The rancher came to life with a blasting roar and his big hands reached for Phil.

His head rocked as Phil's punch banged off his jaw. Phil twisted away, knowing Reiger was an expert at barroom fighting. Trego sidestepped to get clear of Reiger and have a shot at Phil.

A man stepped close just behind Trego. His voice carried sharp and clear. "Stand hitched, Trego."

Trego froze, Colt half drawn. Agren's voice lifted. "I've tied up this buckaroo, Phil. Take care of Reiger."

Reiger charged, head like a battering ram, powerful arms reaching out, stubby fingers hooked. Phil whipped to one side and Reiger wheeled with amazing speed for a man so heavy. His fingers hooked into Phil's arm, but Phil smashed his fist in the man's face and jarred him loose.

For a moment, Reiger's stomach was again exposed. Phil's fist pistoned in just above the belt buckle. Reiger dropped his arm and partially blocked the blow. But his head and chin were wide open. Phil crossed swiftly with his right in a short, chopping blow that cracked off the point of Reiger's chin. The bullet head snapped back and Reiger's hands fell to his sides. He swayed and fell, the jar shaking the building. He lay sprawled on the floor and Phil stood waiting, posed and ready.

But Reiger was out. Agren laughed in triumph. Trego moved, but Agren's Colt muzzle buried deeper in his side.

Trego spoke casually. "You've made a bad mistake, Agren."

"We'll see," Agren chuckled. "You're all right, Phil?"

Phil wiped the sweat from his face, realizing his coat was ripped along one shoulder. He nodded, then stepped to Reiger and shook him until the man's eyes blearily opened. Phil moved back while Reiger slowly rolled over to a sitting position. Suddenly he realized what had happened and he heaved himself to his feet, ready to fight again. Phil felt a grudging respect, but he had sickened of the fight. It proved nothing. He whipped out his gun and leveled it.

Reiger rocked back on his heels, glaring at the black muzzle and then up at Phil. He wiped blood from his nose with the sleeve of his shirt. His voice choked angrily. "Pulling a gun!"

Phil smiled tightly. "You've had your fun, Milt, and you've paid for it. Now you and Dave light out of town."

Reiger glared. "You think this is the end of it?"

"Milt, what's the point? We've had our fight, one that you started. What's the use in acting like a couple of strange bulldogs?" Phil looked at Trego. "Dave, take him home . . . keep him there."

Agren moved his gun along Trego's spine. "You heard him, friend. Why argue?"

Trego stepped up to Reiger. "Come on, Milt. They're holding all the face cards in this deal. Let's head out."

Reiger jerked angrily around and walked away with Trego. He suddenly whirled at the doors and shook his fist at Phil and Agren. "Don't sleep too sound, Ward—and that goes for you, Agren."

They pushed through the batwings and a sigh eased through the crowd. Agren took Phil's arm and swung him to the bar, signaling for drinks.

Phil tossed down his drinks and turned to Agren. "Thanks, Hal. Trego was aching to take a hand."

Agren studied his empty shot glass and sweat stood in little beads on his forehead. He loudly called for another drink, gulped it down. He looked at Phil, his eyes suddenly shadowed. "I guess I didn't make a friend of Trego."

"Nor Reiger," Phil added. "It took nerve to step in like that, Hal."

"Yeah," Agren said tonelessly. He gave Phil a sidelong glance and spoke wryly. "Now where do you suppose I got it?"

IV

It was late afternoon before Fleming sent word that he would visit Phil's office. Phil had long since gone to the little house he had rented in town and changed his ripped clothing. Agren had left him outside the saloon, seemingly in a sudden hurry. He had glanced up and down the street, making sure Reiger and Trego were gone.

The picture remained with Phil and it annoyed him. Naturally, a man would make sure there was no chance of further fight . . . but there had been a hint of something more in Agren's almost frightened—Phil corrected the word—cautious glance. But the picture came back time and again. It wasn't fair to Hal, he thought. He could not forget the way Hal had taken Trego out of the fight. That was not the action of a frightened man.

He had managed to cast it out of his mind by the time Fleming opened the door of the office and looked around with a nod of approval. Tim Moriarty was out supervising the building of the construction camp and there was only Phil and a bookkeeper. Fleming had a huge roll of blueprints under his arm and a pipe in his mouth.

"We'll wait until Mr. Agren gets here," he said. "Some of this will be important to him."

Phil nodded, then said, "I was surprised to meet your sister, Mr. Fleming."

The engineer smiled around the pipe stem. "Carol's been with me for three or four years now. I don't know what I'll do when she leaves."

"She's going somewhere?"

"Not immediately. But she'll find some young man and get married. Since she graduated from school back East, she has been making me a home wherever we travel. I'll rent a place here in Ensign, and within a week or two she'll have it all fixed up. I've gotten used to that."

"I can imagine," Phil said slowly.

Fleming stirred. "What kind of a man is Hal Agren?"

Phil was surprised and cautious until Fleming assured him it had nothing to do with the railroad or the contract. Fleming wanted to know for himself. Phil told what little he knew, giving his own good impressions of the man.

Fleming listened. "He talks rather big."

"Don't hold that against him," Phil laughed. "He acts as big as he talks. Hal will be an important man someday."

"Let's us hope so," Fleming said dryly. "Carol is certainly full of questions about him."

At that moment, Agren breezed into the office and Fleming became all business. He unrolled the prints. They were surveys of the proposed trackage of the Western Pacific, an over-all print followed by each section in the order in which it would be built.

"Phil, these are your copies. Hal, you won't need the prints but you will need to know where and when to deliver the ties. You and Phil will have to work together very closely."

Phil nodded soberly but Agren's laugh boomed out. "Why, Ray, we'll build track faster than you can drive a train across it."

"I'm sure of it," Fleming said, his voice curiously flat. He dropped the back of his hand on the prints. "There's your job, gentlemen. Our rails are beyond Latigo, reaching for Devil's Canyon. That trestle is started. As soon as our rails cross it, we dump everything in your laps. Are you ready for it?"

He listened to their reports of progress. Agren's sawmill was complete except for the machinery, and it was already on its way along with Phil's equipment.

"Better speed it up." Fleming warned. "You haven't much time."

Phil nodded. "We'll see Loman. I'm riding out to the construction camp to make sure it's coming along."

"Good!" Fleming said and looked at Agren.

Hal laughed. "I'm right up to the minute. Timber's being cut right now." He looked at Phil, regret in his face though his eyes held an ill-repressed light. "I'm sorry you're leaving, Phil. I thought you'd have dinner with me—"

"Too busy, Hal," Phil said quickly.

"I know," Agren nodded. He turned to Fleming. "I planned to have you and your charming sister join me, sir. Would it be asking too much?"

"We'd be delighted."

That night, in a lonely camp, Phil pictured Hal Agren with Fleming and his beautiful sister. Here he dined alone on sowbelly and beans while Agren ate in comfort with—he checked the thought and cursed himself. . . .

The next morning Phil headed directly west to the rim of Devil's Canyon, where the trestle would cross. He traversed a small forest of piñon trees through which a road of sorts wound, always following the easiest, rather than the straightest way. The rails would change that as they would change many things in this isolated high country.

He heard the distant sound of hammers, though the trees still hid the camp itself from his sight. Suddenly he jerked erect, hearing the distant echo of a rifle shot. Instantly the pounding ceased. There was another shot, then the silence remained unbroken.

Phil sat motionless for a moment, waiting for the sound of work to resume. But there was a hush, tense and puzzling. He lifted the reins, set spurs to the horse. The animal raced down the twisting ruts, swerving around the trees. Phil broke out into the open. He had a glimpse of the skeletons of the wooden buildings, the roof's triangles of raw lumber against the clear sky. His eyes swept them, searching for trouble. He saw nothing move and realized that there was not a worker in sight.

He raced on, was halfway between the trees and the first of the framed buildings when a bellowing voice arose in a warning shout. "Stay back, ye fool! That sniper—"

The whine of the bullet made him duck and pull back on the reins. The animal came to a sliding halt as another slug split the air just ahead. Phil had a glimpse of a puff of smoke from the distant trees, then he wrenched hard on the reins and set the spurs.

The horse spasmodically jumped in the new direction. Phil heard the report of the rifle but the bullet went wild. He leaned low, raked the spurs again and then the horse reached the broken shelter of the line of buildings. He glimpsed frightened faces looking up at him as he flashed by and realized that the workers had crouched low against the foundations to hide from the sniper.

Phil pulled back on the reins and jumped from the saddle. The buildings, though no more than unfinished framework, now hid him from the trees and the sniper, whoever he was.

Phil jerked his rifle from the boot and wheeled around as Tim Moriarty came lumbering up, his big Irish face dark with anger and worry. His blue eyes swept over Phil and his lips momentarily softened.

"At least the spalpeen missed ye, as he has all the rest."

Phil gestured toward the trees. "Who is that?"

"I'd give the muscles from me right arm to know, bucko," Tim growled. He looked around at the crouching workmen. "It started an hour ago."

"Anyone hurt or—killed?" Phil asked sharply.

Tim took off his hat and scratched his red hair. "Now that is the divil's part of it, lad. 'Tis not a one he has hurt but he has scared the bejasus out of us. There's not a man that'll show himself—and the whole bunch is ready to quit. Here, I'll show ye."

Tim strode to the far, exposed corner of the nearest building. He stood there for a long moment. The distant rifle smacked flatly and splinters flew from the corner studding near Tim's hand. The big Irishman wheeled and stepped out of the line of fire.

"Tim, have you lost your head?" Phil snapped. "You could be killed—"

"Now there you're wrong," Tim cut in. "The black spalpeen has no killing in his dirty mind. But can ye work with lead kicking splinters in your face?"

One of the workers carefully pulled himself up, took a deep breath and then walked to Phil and Tim, his stride tense, as though he would throw himself flat at the first sound. His eyes were round and his face pale.

"Ye'd be quittin'," Tim said scathingly, leaving the man with his mouth hanging open. "It's not in your bones to—"

"Tim," Phil cut in. "I wouldn't blame him if he wants to quit. That's the idea of this sniping. He wants to scare them off."

"But if they won't be scared!" Tim exploded.

"Then he might shoot in earnest," Phil said grimly. "He's just starting. If near misses won't work, maybe a few killed will."

"That's right, Mr. Ward," the worker said swiftly. "We're just carpenters, and we ain't used to being shot at. We'll draw our time and leave before that gent decides to shoot for keeps."

"Wait a minute," Phil cut in. "If I get that man, will you work?"

The man uncertainly looked over at his companions, still crouched low. He finally shrugged. "I don't know about all of them, but I will. It's a good job and I need it."

"Now wait a minute!" Tim shoved forward. "Phil, how would ye be getting at that skulking devil? He can see ye coming before ye start."

"Can you handle a rifle?" Phil asked.

"If we'd had one, it would have been in use long ago."

"Good. Take this one." He shoved it at Tim. "Now lead me to the far end of the buildings."

Tim hefted the rifle, a new light in his eyes, and he plodded away. Phil returned to his horse and followed Tim to the far end of the work area. Just to Phil's left, the empty plain spread toward Devil's Canyon, a few miles away. He could see the railroad survey stakes. Ahead and to his right, the piñon forest started, but the bare area between it and Phil was commanded by the concealed sniper.

"Tim, keep our friend so busy he can't stop me from reaching the trees."

"A pleasure, bucko! And should I happen to puncture the hide of him, I'll not be grieving." Tim hurried along the row of unfinished buildings to the head of the area. He deliberately placed the rifle against a studding and stepped out in the clear view, shaking his fist. "Ye haven't the guts—"

The bullet clipped wood just above his head and Tim jumped back. But he had located the rifleman. With a crooked grin, he bellied down beside the foundation and eased forward so that he had a clear view. Phil swung into saddle when he saw Tim cuddle the rifle to his shoulder.

It cracked and Phil instantly set spurs. He heard the rifle bark again, and a third time, and knew that Tim carefully placed shots in a pattern about the spot where the bushwhacker would be.

The horse made the trees in a burst of speed and no shots were fired at Phil. Once within the shelter of the piñons, he reined the horse in and slid from the saddle. He slipped the Colt from his holster, made a wide swing, and then cautiously drifted in. Tim's rifle cracked constantly and now a second answered it from just ahead. Tim's first shots had caused the man to lay low and Phil knew he had not seen the swift dash of the horse. Otherwise, he would not remain to trade shots with the big Irishman.

Phil worked from tree to tree. Underbrush cut his vision but the sound of the rifles grew steadily louder. He moved more cautiously now. He wanted this man alive. He wanted to find out who sent him and why. Phil had no doubts that Reiger must be somewhere behind this, but he wanted the proof.

Phil cat-footed swiftly to a dense clump of bushes. The rifle was very loud now and he could hear the *snick* as the man ejected a shell after a shot. Phil slowly parted the bushes and peered out.

There was another fringe of bushes, thinner than those behind which Phil hid. Beyond them, he could see the unfinished buildings, then caught the puff of smoke and smack of the rifle as Tim fired again. The bullet splattered dirt several yards to the left of the sniper.

The man himself lay prone. Phil saw scratched boots and soiled Levi's, a faded, checked shirt. The man had pushed back his nondescript hat and Phil could see the dirt in the crumpled circle of the crown. The man's head lowered and Phil knew he sighted along the rifle. Phil eased out of the bushes, Colt leveled.

His voice was low, toneless. "Drop the rifle."

The man jerked and the rifle exploded, the bullet winging off into the sky. Then he dropped the rifle and lay frozen.

"Turn around and get up," Phil ordered. "Keep your hands away from your holster."

The man slowly flexed his legs, half turning. Phil saw a stubbled face, still slack from surprise, and hard black eyes, moist lips set in a taut line below the broken nose. The man came to a crouch, arms extended to support himself.

Phil threw a glance toward the distant buildings. In the split second that his eyes wandered, the man's right hand blurred for his gun and he threw himself twisting to one side as the Colt sprang from the holster.

Phil caught the movement and his finger tightened on the trigger. The gun exploded a split second before the man's. Phil heard the whip of the bullet. The man continued his move to the right but now it was sheer momentum, his body going slack, the gun falling. He sprawled face down, unmoving.

Phil cursed. He touched the shoulder, felt its lifeless weight, and knew the man was dead before he turned him over. The stain on the faded shirt front confirmed it.

Phil slowly stood up and ejected the spent shell from his gun. He stepped through the bushes in full view of the distant buildings and waved his hat over his head. He picked up the ambusher's rifle and returned to the corpse.

By the time Tim Moriarty burst through the screen of bushes, Phil had gone through the man's pockets. The big Irishman looked grimly down at the dead, slack face. "So that's the devil. Who is he?"

"I don't know. Nothing on him." Phil indicated the little pile of coins, yellow cigarette paper, the half-empty sack of makings. "That's it."

"But ye have an idea," Tim said.

Phil nodded. "I have, but how can I prove it? I hoped this jasper would talk."

Tim sighed and looked around. "Where's his horse?"

They found it ground-hitched and masked by a thick copse of bushes. The saddle showed hard usage and had no marks except the crude letters "A.E." cut on the underside of one of the stirrups. The horse wore two brands, one of them vented, but both of them unknown to Phil.

He pulled the dangling reins over the animal's head and spoke in discouragement. "A saddle tramp with his gun and rifle for hire. We'll wrap him up and I'll take him in to the sheriff. Make any bets that someone will know him?"

Tim shook his head. "That I will not. The black imp who hired him will be as innocent as the rest." He shrugged his big shoulders. "But this is not building a camp. I'll tell those fainthearted buckos back there that they'll be bothered no more."

V

The next day Phil left the construction camp, leading the horse with the canvas-covered body roped across the saddle. The next saddle tramp with a ready rifle would be stopped before he started. The ride back to Ensign seemed to be endless. There was so much to do and Phil felt the pressure of time.

There was a brief flurry in the town when he rode down the main street to the sheriff's office, leading the horse with its grim burden. Sheriff Jere Miles took a look at the dead man and then had his deputy take the body to the undertaker. The crowd broke up when Jere led Phil into his office.

Phil told him all he knew. Jere, a leather-faced man with shaggy white brows, looked sharply at him. "So you never saw him before, but you've got an idea who sent him."

"No proof," Phil answered.

"Maybe I can get it."

"How?" Phil demanded. "No one will admit knowing this man, or ever having met him before. You'll waste your time, Jere."

"But something has to be done!" the lawman exploded.

"I'm sending some of the Flying W boys to the

construction camp. There won't be any more sniping."

Miles grunted. "Every citizen has a right to protect himself and his property."

Phil went to the engineer's office and found that Fleming and his sister had left Ensign. One of the men grinned. "That Agren sure buzzes around Miss Fleming—and she likes it, too. He invited Ray and his sister to inspect his timber holdings. They'll be gone a couple of days."

It was a disappointment, for Phil had hoped to have at least another glimpse of Carol. He recalled Hal Agren's flat statement that he intended to sweep Carol off her feet. It looked as though he would do exactly that. . . .

The next morning Phil rode northward toward his Flying W spread. Once on the familiar trail, he felt the tension and worries of the last few days leave him. He set the horse at an easy pace, glad of this chance to find his balance again.

As Phil drew rein and swung out of the saddle, Farrell, his foreman came lounging up to the corral. Farrell looked sharply at him, thumbed his hat back from a high, tanned forehead. "Hope you stay around a time, Phil. Looks like you need it. Moriarty handles things at the camp, and that equipment ain't due for a few days. Spend the time here."

Phil was persuaded. There were many things that needed his attention, from work on the books to sending half a dozen armed men to Tim Moriarty at the construction camp. There were long rides with Farrell over the range to check the herds. It was good to ride free from the bustle of Ensign and all the problems that had flooded in on him of late.

They made a great circle about headquarters, camping at night, and then their path brought them close to the Lazy R line. Phil saw a couple of strange riders at a distance.

Farrell also saw them and frowned. "Cutting across our range. There's been a lot of that lately."

Phil eyed the distant riders. "Reiger's men?"

"I think so. They have that be-damned, gunhung look of the Lazy R bunch."

"Any trouble?"

"No," Farrell answered slowly. "No cows missing. None of 'em bother our boys any. It makes me edgy, though."

Phil nodded. "Reiger has that contract in his craw. I don't like it, either."

"We could drive 'em off Flying W range when we meet 'em," Farrell suggested.

Phil considered this. The distant riders had disappeared in a draw, still riding steadily toward Lazy R. Phil slowly shook his head. "No—not yet, anyhow. It could lead to gunplay. If Reiger could involve the Flying W in a range war, we'd never be able to meet the beef commitments."

"Maybe he plans that anyhow," Farrell said

grimly. "Funny thing about these wandering jaspers—they always ride close to our beef gathers, looking them over."

"Leave 'em alone," Phil decided. "If they make a wrong play, that's something else, but we don't want to fall into any trap Reiger might set."

Farrell nodded. "I'll tell the boys."

They gradually swung away from Lazy R and approached the timberlands where Hal Agren cut his railroad ties. They camped that night and, early the next morning, they reached the southern boundary of Flying W and headed eastward. Suddenly Farrell reined in and looked closely at the ground. "Two more of 'em, Phil. Just ahead somewhere. Came out of the woods."

"Let's see what they have to say," Phil snapped.

They spurred along the trail and Phil saw that these two would pass very close to the ranch big house. Bold enough, he thought angrily. They dipped into a swale and the trail veered eastward. They came around a turn and saw the two horsemen some distance away.

Phil saw that one seemed exceptionally slender. Suddenly that one looked back and instantly drew rein. The other rider also turned and they stood waiting. Phil caught a glimpse of golden hair under a broad-brimmed hat, and recognized Carol Fleming. The other rider was her brother.

In a few moments he reined in before them, surprised and delighted. Carol wore a blouse and a split riding skirt, the slender waist circled by a belt worked in Indian silver. The ride had put high color in her cheeks.

"We were coming to visit you," she said.

Fleming nodded. "Since we were this close to Flying W, I wanted to take a look at the source of our beef supply."

"You're sure welcome," Phil blurted. "I didn't expect this."

"Neither did I," Carol said, "but Rayburn makes quick decisions."

Phil looked beyond them, back to Carol. "Is Hal along?"

"No," she said and Phil instantly caught the ring of disappointment in her tone. "He couldn't come—some minor trouble at the camp."

Phil nodded and introduced Farrell, and then the four continued the journey to the ranch. Carol gave an exclamation of delight when she first saw the rambling, rough beauty of the ranch house, the neat, white corrals, the barns and buildings, clean and inviting. She was even more pleased when Phil ushered her and Rayburn into the big main room. She walked to the fireplace and turned and looked slowly about at the Navajo blankets making bright splashes against the dark logs of the wall, up at the beamed ceiling, at the windows that looked out on the distant hills.

"It's a dream, Phil! It's something you should share."

"I'd like to," he said quickly, "some time . . . when the right person comes along."

She was startled, then flushed and laughed, turned to her brother. "She'll be lucky, won't she?"

Rayburn nodded and Carol continued to look about the room. But Phil sensed she had told him she was not the "right person." He hid his disappointment and then caught Rayburn's shrewd, keen appraisal. Phil sent Farrell to the cook with a request for a special dinner. He poured a drink for Rayburn and coffee for Carol; they sat in the big leather chairs before the fireplace.

Carol was filled with the wonders of the lumber camp. Phil sensed that she felt that Hal Agren would undoubtedly become the greatest man in this area. Phil wryly wondered why he did not have Hal's gift of self-praise.

Then Rayburn asked to see the cattle count and Phil took him to the office. The engineer looked at the tallies, nodding, then shot shrewd questions at Phil.

"No worry here, then," he said, leaning back in the desk chair. "Hal is doing well, too."

"You spent some time with him?" Phil asked casually.

"Yes. A couple of days. An impressive man, Hal Agren."

"He'll go far," Phil nodded.

"He's persuaded Carol, at least," Fleming said dryly. He glanced at Phil. "I thought at first we might see more of you."

Phil shrugged. "It didn't work that way."

"I know," Fleming arose from the desk and, at the door, he paused. "Carol's already taken with your home, Phil. I hope she has a pleasant time."

The Flemings spent the afternoon and night at the Flying W. The cook outdid himself and Carol was interested in everything she saw when Phil took her on a tour. They started back to the house.

"You're young, Phil, to own all this."

He laughed. "Sure, but I didn't start from the bottom. My father owns a big business in San Francisco, but after working a time as a puncher, I knew I wanted to ranch." He shrugged. "I bought Flying W and built it up."

"A lot of work and imagination has gone into it." She sighed. "Hal has the same dreams, but in a different field, of course."

"He's told me," Phil nodded. "A good man."

"The best," she said with a smile.

Phil gave her a sidelong glance. She was certainly all he had ever dreamed of in a woman, but he could see that he had lost the race before it was begun. "You like Hal a lot."

She looked around, startled, then smiled. "You miss very little, Phil. Yes, I do."

"Then I wish you the best—both of you."

She laughed, then sobered. "He hasn't asked me yet, Phil. But I'm sure he will."

They returned to the house. The rest of the stay was pleasant enough, and yet it was a strain. Carol's constant presence drove home to him that Hal Agren had won her loyalty as well as her love. . . .

The next morning, Phil rode back to Ensign with them. They arrived in the town late in the afternoon and Phil left them before the small, neat cottage Fleming had rented. Carol thanked him with a warm handshake that bothered Phil more than he cared to admit.

He rode on to his office, where the bookkeeper said that Will Loman reported the equipment was nearing Devil's Canyon. Tim Moriarty had sent word that the work camp construction was nearly done.

Both bits of news gave Phil a new lift, and he realized how much Agren's progress with Carol had depressed him. But that was over and done now, he knew. He moved restlessly about the office. He wondered if Loman had sent word to Agren about the shipment. He walked down the busy street, turned off and climbed the short, steep slope to Agren's sawmill. The building was ready. There remained only the installation of boilers and saw equipment, and the place would hum.

Phil climbed up on the platform and his boots echoed on the wide boards as he approached the office. Just as he reached for the door, it opened and Agren stopped short in surprise.

"You!" he said and there was quick anger in his tone.

Phil regarded him in mild puzzlement. "Sure, Hal."

Agren blocked the doorway, eyes cold and boring. "I'd not expect you to show up here."

Phil straightened. "Hal, what's eating you?"

"As if you didn't know! I don't like people going behind my back—"

"For what!" Phil demanded, angry.

"You've been with Carol for two days now. I didn't want her to go to Flying W, but Fleming insisted." Agren's eyes narrowed. "I guess you hadn't put any pressure on him."

Phil stared, angry, and then the ludicrousness of it struck him. He laughed. "Man, you're eaten up with jealousy! Not that I blame you. Carol's a beautiful woman."

"And you—" Hal started hotly.

"I know I haven't a chance," Phil cut in. "She made it very clear there was someone else—you."

Hal searched his face, suspicion slowly leaving him. "She said that?"

"She did, Hal. So we had a nice visit, and it ended there. Hal, once you've won a girl like Carol, you never have to worry about her. She's loyal."

Hal bit his lip. He rubbed his fingers along his

jaw and then grinned apologetically. "You're right, Phil. Come in. What's on your mind?"

Phil mentioned the equipment and its probable route. "Circling Devil's Canyon, it'll come close to my work camp. I'll have my wagons turn off there. I thought maybe you'd like to get a first look at your sawmill stuff, so ride out with me."

"Sure!" Hal exclaimed. "I'll get the boys ready to install it the minute it comes."

Phil nodded. "Early tomorrow. It'll be a long ride."

He left. Agren walked to the window and looked out. He rocked back and forth on heels and toes, hands thrust deep in his pockets. He smiled softly, considering how much marriage to Carol would mean.

But then Agren's eyes narrowed. Had he been told all the truth? If he had been Ward and had been rebuffed by Carol, he would not give up so easily, no matter what he might say. He'd work carefully, but always tell the other fellow half-truths to keep him smug and off guard.

Agren frowned. It was too damn good to be true. Ward planned to keep him blind and infatuated with his apparent success, while he slowly undermined Carol's regard. That was it.

He grunted. "A cold day in hell, Phil Ward, when I'm pulled in!"

The next morning Phil, mounted, waited impatiently for Agren to join him. At last Hal broke out of the stream of traffic and reined in beside him. He greeted Phil on a warm and friendly note. With a nod, Phil turned his horse and both men rode out of town.

They cut far south, crossed to the east rim of Devil's Canyon, and rode steadily northward to meet the caravan of freight wagons. They had seen them the day before, but the great chasm of the canyon had allowed them only to shout to the drivers across the gorge.

In midafternoon they met the caravan. The trail boss grinned at their eagerness, squinting up at the sun. "Reckon we won't get much further today, anyhow. We'll make camp and you can take a look. Here's the manifests."

He extended papers to Phil. Agren eagerly received his own lists. They read them over as the head teamster ordered camp to be made.

The wagons were swung around to within a few yards of the canyon rim and parked in a long row, brakes set and boulders chunked under the rear wheels. The teams were unhitched and picketed some distance away from the wagons and the big campfire where the teamsters cooked their supper and then lolled, smoking and talking. Phil and Agren had looked under the wagon tarps, saw the gleam of scraper blades, the scoop-like shape of the drags.

The night wore on and the teamsters rolled up in blankets to get some needed rest. Phil hugged his knees and stared thoughtfully into the embers half listening to Hal's swift, sure talk of the things he planned, now that he had actually seen his mill machinery. "Your boys had better place ties fast, Phil, or I'll be stacking wood from here to the Colorado."

Phil laughed. "I think Tim can get the men who'll make you run to keep up with us."

"Now do you want to make a bet about—"

A wild, screeching yell cut him short, and then a blast of gunfire swept just over their heads. Pounding hoofs thundered close in the outer darkness. Blankets erupted as frightened teamsters came to their feet and stared wildly about. Agren sat frozen, face slack until Phil grabbed his arm and yelled above the din.

"Get your rifle! This is—"

His voice was drowned by another blast of gunfire. Agren scrambled after him as Phil raced to his saddle and the scabbard that held his rifle. Agren fumbled for his weapon, finally drew it from the scabbard.

Now wild riders plunged into the camp and guns blasted, bloodcurdling screeches lifted into the night. The teamsters broke and ran, creating a milling chaos sweeping like a rushing tide over Phil and Agren and carrying them into headlong flight.

Phil tried to break loose but he was pushed along until he finally worked his way to the edge of the fleeing group and was free. He gasped for breath, dashed sweat from his eyes, then looked back toward the camp.

Gunfire still pursued the flying teamsters, but all the shots were high. Obviously these attackers would not kill unless they had to. By the light of the distant fire, Phil saw men scurrying about, but there was a definite purpose to their swift movements. Suddenly Agren, winded and blowing, appeared at Phil's side.

"For God's sake! What is it?" he demanded. "Robbers?"

"Of a wagon train carrying machinery?" Phil snapped. "They'd spend their time on a gold box on a stagecoach. There's something else here."

"And a hell of a lot of 'em!" Agren said jerkily.

Phil peered toward the fire and the wagons. The attackers moved with precision, vaulting from their saddles and running to the big wagons. Phil heard the dull thud of rocks dropping into the deep canyon.

At the same moment, some of the men bent to the big wheels, straining against them. Others remained on their horses, facing out to the darkness, Colts held ready, the firelight gleaming wickedly from their barrels.

Phil sucked in his breath. "Hal! They'll roll the wagons into the gorge! Our equipment—"

He snapped the rifle to his shoulder.

VI

Agren grabbed the gun and forced it down. Phil turned savagely, saw the strained, white blur of Agren's face. The man's voice was choked. "Phil! Don't shoot! They'll gun us down."

Phil tried to jerk the rifle free of the clutching grasp. "You fool! Want our stuff in the bottom of Devil's Canyon! It's fight now or lose it all."

Agren's hand dropped from the rifle. Phil gestured toward the camp. "Pick off the men at the wagon wheels."

"The riders?" Agren asked uncertainly, but he had lifted his rifle.

"Forget them. Get the men at the wheels—now!"

He took a quick aim and fired. The bullet sang off a broad wagon rim within an inch of a man's nose. The renegade jumped back and Phil swung the rifle to another man. It cracked again. The man clutched a shoulder.

Agren's rifle fired. His shooting was ragged and his aim poor, but splinters sprayed from the high wagon beds. The mounted men wheeled and Colts blasted, the bullets whipping high over their heads. Phil took time to snap a bullet at the guards and a man dropped his gun, grabbing the saddlehorn as the horse raced away.

Phil grimly pumped shots at the attackers clearly outlined by the fire. Horses squealed in the darkness and there was pandemonium throughout the camp. Agren lifted the hat from one man's head, sent a second spinning about and stumbling off.

Their fire was too concentrated for the band. One man spurred his horse toward them, but the next second he sailed backward over the saddle as Phil's slug caught him. The rest broke and raced away.

As swiftly as it had started, it ended. One moment firelight touched on the milling, shooting men. The next moment they were gone and the fading pound of hoofs told of their swift retreat. Phil slowly lowered his weapon.

Agren moistened his lips. "Think—they're gone?"

Phil nodded. "And just in time. Let's take a look."

He led the way, Agren cautiously trailing him. One man lay sprawled several yards from the fire where Phil's bullet had spilled him from the saddle. Phil gave a sweeping glance at the wagons, saw that only one or two had been moved a scant foot or so. Then he bent over the man on the ground.

Agren hovered close as Phil looked down at the dead man. He had the same pinched, hard-faced mark of the sniper Phil had shot beyond the construction camp. Maybe another saddle bum without identification, Phil thought grimly, and started through his pockets.

He dimly heard the cautious sound of the returning teamsters as they formed a silent circle around him. He looked up at the boss teamster. "You boys get around all over this country. Know him?"

Phil's eyes cut sharply from driver to driver. Each shook his head. The boss scratched the rasping stubble of his jaw. "Don't remember him at all, Ward. Looks like maybe a hundred I've seen one time or the other, but—"

"Gunhawk and renegade," Phil said flatly. "You can always spot them." He sighed and stood up.

The boss gestured out toward the dark. "I don't savvy why they'd jump a train like this. Ain't nothing worthwhile to a bunch of renegades."

"Your mistake," Phil answered. "It was worth something to them to pitch the wagons over the rim. They don't like grading and sawmill equipment."

Phil explained his suspicions. He held back Reiger's name, feeling it would not be wise to mention it. The teamsters listened and then shifted uneasily, glancing again toward the dark beyond the reach of the fire.

"I don't think they'll be back," Phil said. "They lost one man and a couple more picked up bullets. They know we'll be waiting for them. You can rest easy."

"Sure," one of the men answered, "down under them wagons where the shadows are black and no one can see us. Me, I'll be glad to be rid of this load."

The others growled assent and Phil moved away. Hal Agren had given the wagons a close examination and now he stood at the end of the row, waiting for Phil.

"Bullet holes in some of them," he said, "but no damage to the cargo. Boilers and scrapers are hard to puncture." He shook his head. "I hope nothing like this happens again."

Phil caught the faint trace of fear still about Hal's eyes and mouth. "It won't—for now. But Reiger won't stop until we can get the proof to slap him in a cell."

"Reiger?" Agren asked.

"Remember his threats at Latigo? Remember the fight in town? He's determined to ruin me if he can't have that contract."

Agren glanced down the line of giant wagons and cleared his throat. "But—some of this is *my* equipment. I didn't take any contract from him."

"Reiger's seen us work together. You held Trego out of that fight. He figures to hit both of us." He looked around at the men who now brewed coffee at the fire. "Nothing more we can do now, I guess. We'll take Reiger's renegade to Ensign and give him to Jere Miles."

They rolled up in their blankets again, Agren to

sleep with the teamsters while Phil sat beyond the reach of firelight, his rifle over his knees. There was no further attack and, when dawn revealed the barren land, no sign of a renegade band except for the hoof-churned earth around the wagons.

Breakfast was a silent, withdrawn meal. Now and then Phil caught a teamster covertly regarding him, frowning and a touch fearful. Agren ate thoughtfully and with reluctance, joined Phil at the head of the caravan.

They came to the place where the direct trail to Phil's construction camp split off from the main Ensign road. Some of the wagons took the cutoff, Phil leading them. Agren continued on to Ensign with his sawmill equipment and the dead renegade, tarp-rolled, in one of the wagons.

Moriarty had his men help place the graders and scoops along the survey stakes. The spades, picks and shovels were stored in a warehouse. At last the empty wagons rolled away and the lead teamster grinned crookedly at Phil. "The next time you got something coming this way, send for the cavalry. It's wearing to be shot at."

Phil went with Moriarty to the rim of Devil's Canyon. He looked in amazement at the trestle that already reached across the chasm. Workers swarmed over it and Phil saw that it would be quickly finished. Tim pointed across the chasm.

"And rail is coming fast, bucko. 'Tis high time I filled them bunkhouses with workers."

Phil nodded. "Right away."

He left the camp early the next morning and rode toward Ensign with a thousand things on his mind. The town seemed more crowded. He saw strange faces as he rode along where a few months before almost everyone had been familiar. The greater part of the influx seemed to be laborers, but Phil also noticed several men in the typical dark coat and string tie of the gambler, their eyes sharp and predatory, belaying their suave manners and soft speech. He knew that such birds of prey must inevitably follow the railroad boomtowns and construction camps.

He dismounted before the sheriff's office. Jere Miles sat with his boot heels up on the desk, his heavy face tired. From the cell section came the off-key, tremulous voice of a drunken song and Phil glanced that way.

Miles grunted. "This place is getting crowded. The railroad's going to change the town, Phil."

"I know." Phil sank down in the chair across the desk. "It'll bring trouble as well as blessings."

"Speaking of which, you sent trouble in wrapped in canvas. Making a collection of dead saddle tramps?"

"Hal told you the story and my suspicions?"

"Both, for what it was worth. No one knew the son, and Reiger got ringy when I questioned

77

him. I asked where his crew was the other night."

"What'd he say?"

"Why, they stayed real close to the Lazy R bunkhouse. Reiger can prove it—by the men themselves, of course, one swearing a lie about the other. Dared me to do something about it."

Phil took off his hat and dropped it on the floor. "Nothing can be done, but I wanted to clear things with you anyhow."

Miles considered his blunt fingers. "How long you going to take this sort of thing, Phil?"

"I don't know. Until I can get some proof that will let me turn you loose on Reiger and the Lazy R."

"The way it's going," Miles commented, "you could go belly-up on that railroad contract and be dead broke by the time it happened."

"Worse, Miles. Ruined's the word." He grinned as he pulled himself to his feet. "But I think there might be some fighting before that happens."

The next two weeks sped by in a haze of work, problems, and snap decisions. He ordered Farrell to drive the first small herd toward the camp and Agren, meeting him for a rare quarter-hour of relaxation in one of the saloons, asked that Phil speed up beef shipments to his camps.

"Good," Phil nodded, and smiled apologetically. "I've been so busy, I can't see beyond my own problems."

"Fleming told me last night at supper."

"How's Carol?" Phil asked.

Agren signaled for another drink. He lifted his glass. "To Carol. She'll be my wife."

Phil's spirits sagged. "You've asked her? She's accepted?"

"Well, I'm waiting for the right moment, Phil. But she'll say yes. You can tell about those things."

After Agren walked away, Phil had the strong impulse to go to the Fleming cottage. But what could he say to Carol? He looked at his image in the bar mirror and made a mocking toast to his reflection. Then he walked out. There was a mountain of work waiting at the office.

Tim Moriarty came riding in the next day and Phil expected the office to be filled with the wanderers who had come here for jobs. But the big Irishman let them collect outside, and when he judged there were enough of them, he picked about fifty men and dismissed the rest. He took the names of those he had chosen and came back in the office, satisfied.

Phil regarded him, puzzled. "Is that all? You've hired only a drop in the bucket to what we'll need."

Tim grinned, "Ye'd be forgetting as soon as the contractor east of here reaches Devil's Canyon, his job is done. He has a full crew of experienced men. I've hired all of 'em that still want to work on the railroad. We only pick up the extras here. . . ."

A week later, Phil rode out to the construction camp. Beyond his own camp stretched a new area and he stared at the swiftly rising buildings, frowned and then rode directly to the camp office. Tim Moriarty laughed when he asked about the new area. "Phil, ye have looked upon end-of-track. 'Tis the honkytonk town that follows the railroad. This one has moved, step by step, all the way from Kansas. It'll keep on moving until the rails touch the Pacific Ocean. Here, I'll show ye."

He picked up his hat and led the way outside. Phil was amazed to see, beyond the canyon, that the rails had almost reached the rim. He listened to the clang of hammers on spikes and rails. The trestle itself was completed and men placed rails across it, ready to hook in to the steel that greedily reached for it.

"There'll be no break in the work," Tim said. "The bunch over there places the last bit of steel, crosses the trestle and lays steel on this side— but on our payroll." He jerked his thumb over his shoulder. "And now we'll visit our new neighbors. 'Tis an education ye'll be having."

He led the way to the new area. Phil's eyes moved on down the street, from building to building. "Saloons—and dancehalls!"

"Right," Tim nodded. "Ye'll find that most of

80

the money ye pay the workers will be spent right here. When we move, they will move."

Phil studied the street. As he watched, men erected a long sign over a nearby building. "Pennard's High Iron," he read aloud. A little further along another sign announced that the Golden Wheel had roulette, chuck-a-luck, faro and poker. Beyond it stood a huge tent saloon.

"Later," Tim said, "there'll be a side street. Ye'll find the girls there."

He started away, but Phil checked him. "Let's take a look at one of these places."

Tim caught a shadow of anger about Phil's jaw. He sobered. "Phil, end-of-track is as necessary as supplies. A man works hard six days a week. The seventh day, he wants the taste of beer or whisky, the chance of a gamble, the look of a woman. If he doesn't have it, he quits. Leave this place be if ye want a railroad."

Phil led the way to Pennard's. He saw two saddled horses ground-hitched at the far corner. He crossed the porch and entered a doorway where the batwings had not as yet been hung. The interior was huge. A long bar stood at one side, on the other were stacked tables and chairs. Behind the bar, two men worked at stacking bottles of whisky. From the rear came the pound of a hammer.

One of the men behind the bar saw them, grinned, and asked their pleasure. Before Phil could answer, Tim ordered drinks. Tim and the bartender talked, the man saying they would be filled with customers by tomorrow when the crew crossed the trestle. "From then on, we'll hum—like we always have."

Phil placed his glass on the bar. "Gambling, too?"

"Sure, soon as the layouts are set up."

"Straight games?" Phil asked sharply. "I'll have nothing else around my camps, and honest whisky. Otherwise, you'll close."

"I will!" a harsh voice demanded behind him. "By whose orders?"

Phil wheeled around to face a short, stocky man with coarse, arrogant features and sallow skin. He rolled a cigar around between thick lips. "No one tells Joe Pennard."

Phil shook his head. "Your mistake, Pennard. I'm Phil Ward and this is my construction camp. You run a straight, decent place or you close."

Some of the certainty left Pennard's face: "No one has accused me of anything wrong yet."

There was a stir and Phil looked beyond Pennard's shoulder. A door had opened onto what would be Pennard's office, and Milt Reiger stood framed in it. Dave Trego eased out behind Milt as the man came into the room. Reiger stopped a few feet away, thumbs hooked in his gunbelt. Trego slipped like a dark shadow to one side and waited. Reiger's mean eyes held Phil for a moment and then cut to Pennard.

"You listen real careful to Mr. Ward, Joe. You can't tell when he'll sneak up behind your back and pull some crooked deal."

Tim stirred, but Phil made a swift gesture to check him. He disregarded Reiger, and his eyes locked with Pennard's. Two more men, wearing guns, materialized out of the shadows. This would make a perfect gun trap.

"No argument, Pennard," Phil snapped, "unless you run the wrong kind of place. Everyone else will be told the same thing. You can write it down as a new rule."

He nodded coldly, and his eyes lifted to Reiger, swept him with a contemptuous glance. Then he turned on his heel and strode out. Tim followed him and, on the porch stopped dead when Reiger's loud voice carried clearly.

"You heard him, Joe! Don't do nothing to set that sidewinder against you. He won't meet you straight out, but he sneaks—"

Phil's voice cut in. "Tim! Let it be! They want a fight! Think we'd have a chance?"

He managed to get the big Irishman off the porch and down on the street. Phil strode away, his eyes angry.

Tim caught up with him. " 'Twould be little chance we'd have. But ye'll have a real shootout with that spalpeen if he don't bushwhack you first."

"No bet," Phil said shortly. "It's a sure thing."

VII

When Phil returned to Ensign and his office, Fleming had left word that there would be a final meeting at his house tonight. The thought of having another short visit with Carol, even though others would be present, took the unpleasantness of the meeting with Reiger from Phil's mind.

After a lonely supper, he dressed for the evening, taking particular care. It was dark by the time he started the short walk. He soon saw the friendly lights of the cottage on the street ahead. As he came up, a horseman approached, drew rein and dismounted.

Hal Agren spoke cheerfully to Phil and ground-tied his horse. They strode up the walk together. Light blazed as the cottage door opened and Carol looked out with eager welcome, Agren sprang ahead and took her hand. She looked up at him, smiling softly, and then turned to Phil.

"You're welcome. Ray's waiting inside."

Agren held her hand. "I didn't come to see just Ray."

She laughed, pleased. "It will not all be business. We'll have coffee and cake as soon as you men have finished your discussion."

Still holding Agren's hand, she led the way inside. Phil followed, wondering why he hadn't pushed as hard as Agren and talked as boldly.

Fleming again had blueprints and surveys spread out on the big table in the center of the dining room. He shook hands with Phil, nodded to Agren as he would a constant visitor and indicated chairs. He looked at Agren, then at Phil, as though making a final check of his impression of them. Carol quietly left the room, closing the door. Fleming hitched up to the table and dropped his hand on the prints.

"The rails cross the Devil's Canyon tomorrow," he said without preliminary. "That means your real work begins. Starting tomorrow, your penalty clauses will operate."

"Why, Ray," Agren cut in, "I can't think of anything that can go wrong."

"You, Phil?" Fleming turned suddenly.

"I'm ready, but who can tell what will come up? I'll do my best to meet any problem."

Fleming nodded, pleased. "Hal, you might borrow from Phil's book. In this game, you can't be sure of anything."

Agren flushed and shot a swift glance at Phil, irritation swiftly masked. Fleming turned to the surveys, pointed out places where they might have trouble, suggested means of speeding the work. Phil was surprised to find that over two hours had sped by when Fleming finally rolled the maps and sighed in relief.

"Well, there it is. It's coffee time."

Carol came in with coffee and slices of cake. Agren managed to monopolize most of Carol's time, as though he feared Phil might speak to the girl.

At last it was time to go. Fleming pushed his cup aside and again looked at the two. He smiled faintly. "I hope you both remember this. It'll probably be your last carefree night until we reach the Colorado."

Agren nodded. "I know, but we'll make it. I'm leaving at dawn to make sure my camps start full schedule. You'll get your ties, all right."

"Good!" Fleming smiled. "But that's Phil's problem."

Phil laughed. "Tim Moriarty says he can lay every tie and rail that's placed beside the right of way. I'll leave in the morning, too, to start the grading. We join with the Devil's Canyon rails."

Fleming nodded, glanced at Carol. "Like company, Phil?"

"Of course!" Phil looked up, startled.

"Good. If you don't mind, Carol and I will drive out with you. Got a place to put us up?"

"If we haven't, we'll make a place," Phil laughed.

Agren cut in angrily. "I don't think a construction camp is a place for a girl. I—"

"Nonsense!" Fleming snapped. "Carol's been to camps before. I need her to drive me, and I have to be there as chief engineer."

Agren's lips set and his fingers tightened into fists. He caught himself and turned to Carol. "You think you should go?"

"Of course," Fleming cut in. "Hal, you'll be gone for a day or two. You'll be too busy to miss us."

Agren tried to smile, but didn't succeed very well. His speech became short, almost curt. Phil saw that Carol was upset and annoyed. Fleming arose and Phil thanked Carol, shook hands with Fleming and turned to Agren, smiling. "I guess you'll stay for a while."

"I'll walk to the street with you."

Phil again said good night to Carol but she hardly heard him, her worried attention on Agren. The two young men walked out to the street and Agren waited until the door had closed behind them.

He instantly swung to Phil. "I don't like this!"

Phil choked back his anger. "Hal, I didn't invite them. What can I do?"

Agren grunted. "Tell them you're too busy."

"Fleming's chief engineer. Can I tell him to go someplace else! You act as though you think I planned this."

"Maybe you did."

Phil's irritation broke. "You're a jealous fool, Hal! I think you need a lesson. I'll see you when I get back. Good night."

The next day, Fleming and Carol riding beside

him, Phil did not set too fast a pace toward the distant construction camp. All too soon they came to the camp. The place bustled and end-of-track boomed and roared. They went first to the camp office, learning that Tim Moriarty was out at the trestle, watching the rails from the eastern side swiftly close the small gap to the bridge.

Fleming's eyes lighted. "I want to see this myself."

They headed toward the canyon along a well defined road formed by the passage of wagons, horses and men. The spanning of the chasm had drawn everyone from the camp and end-of-track. Now and then they gave way for empty freight wagons, returning for more material and tools.

Fleming nodded approval. "Leave it to Big Tim to be ready to jump."

The western rim of the canyon was a seething mass of workers, onlookers, laborers ready to begin work the moment the signal was given. Already scrapers and graders formed the first section of the roadbed and dust rose in a choking cloud.

Phil forced a path to the very edge of the canyon and the western end of the completed trestle. Tim Moriarty barked orders that set the crews to faster work. The roadbed seemed to form under Phil's eyes, reaching westward between the surveyors' stakes.

Carol gasped when she looked into the canyon.

It was deep, rocky and grim, the bottom narrow and forbidding. But the trestle spanned it, reached down to solid rock foundation. Beyond, on the eastern bank, men placed ties and great steel rails, lifted from work cars, were put in place. The gauger took but a moment and then sledges rang on spikes even as more ties and rails were placed ahead.

The work and supply train moved slowly forward. Steel fingers reached out, touched and were joined with the steel already placed on the trestle. Instantly a great cheer arose.

Phil stood beside Tim who turned, broad face beaming. " 'Tis done! Ye'll be the first to step aboard the train that crosses the canyon." His bull roar lifted above the noise. "Ties! Place 'em, ye terriers! Sweat! Build a railroad!"

Swiftly the first string of ties was put in place. Across the canyon, the work train blew a long whistle blast and then crept forward, shoving the flat cars of rails across the trestle, easing to a halt just short of the western bank. Men swarmed over the car and rails eased out and off, a crew of men receiving their weight and grunting as they placed them.

Phil watched with mounting excitement as the gauger made adjustments and sledges again rang on spikes and fish plates were set. This was on *his* side of the canyon. The responsibility for the Western Pacific was now his.

Track snaked forward with unbelievable rapidity. Gradually the line extended until there was room enough for the train to stand on this side of the canyon. Then work ceased.

Tim turned with a wide grin to Phil, and then looked at Fleming. "The train will pull back to make the first formal crossing. It would be a fine thing did both ye ride the engine, knowing ye've whipped Devil's Canyon."

Phil's face lighted and Fleming nodded eagerly. Phil took Carol's arm. "You'll ride with us, the first girl to take a train in this part of Arizona!"

They swung aboard the engine, the crew giving them wide, soot-streaked grins. The diamond-stacked locomotive backed across the trestle and picked up speed to a siding, where it cut loose the work cars. The engineer gave a long blast and the locomotive, free of its burden, sped westward again. Phil hung onto a stanchion and Carol clung to his arm. He stole a glance at her excited, flushed face and hastily looked away.

The rails and the trestle gleamed in the sunlight, a steel arrow that crossed the land and darted through the black mass of humanity on the far bank. They slowly crossed the trestle. Carol looked out and down, gasped, and clutched tightly at Phil's arm. It was as though there was nothing between them and the jagged rocks far below.

Then the whistle made a deafening blast and the sound of the wheels changed as the locomotive rolled onto solid land. With a hiss of steam and a screech of brakes it jerked to a halt, the last of the rails just ahead. The blasting continued as the crowd shouted, hats tossed in the air. The defeat of Devil's Canyon had been formally accomplished.

Even as Phil swung down from the cab and assisted Carol to descend, he heard the shouts of the graders at work beyond the rails. The crowd broke up, the greater part moving purposively to the roadbed with shovel and pick. Many headed for the end-of-track honkytonks.

The locomotive, with a short warning blast, moved back across the trestle. Fleming came to Phil, smiling and extending his hand. "Phil, the railroad is now yours. We'll bring over the steel. The rest is up to you."

"He'll do a good job, Ray." Carol smiled at Phil, excitement dancing in her eyes. "But before you settle down to labor, Phil, show me around."

Soon they rode side by side through the camp, Phil leading the way to some of the pleasant forest trails. He felt the nearness of the woman but tried to act as though she was a good friend and no more. Still, his thoughts were in a turmoil. He fought them down, but they returned with renewed strength. After a long circuit, they came again to the gorge of Devil's Canyon, far north of the trestle. They crossed a sunny expanse of long grass bending to the wind and reined in a few feet from the canyon rim.

Carol looked slowly around the horizon. Phil watched her, noting the soft curves of her lovely body, the proud lift of chin, the soft lips, the way her hair curled about her slender shoulders. He bit at his lips and considered the reins in his hands.

"Phil, it's lovely!" she said. "I'm so glad I came!"

"So am I." He spoke quickly and a startled change in her expression let him know that he had revealed something of his own thoughts. He kept tight rein on his voice. "I'll never forget this ride with you."

"I—thanks, Phil."

He lifted the reins. "Shall we get back to camp?"

A short distance away, screened by the trees and bushes, Reiger and Trego sat their horses and watched the man and woman ride off. They remained motionless until Phil and Carol had disappeared. Then they talked excitedly for a moment, reined about, and rode toward Ensign.

VIII

Phil returned to Ensign with Fleming and Carol. In a way, he was glad to part with them, for the girl's nearness, after the ride to the rim of the canyon, was something of a torture. He had to steel himself against the touch of her hand when she thanked him for the trip.

He plunged into work that afternoon and immediately learned the real pressure of building a railroad. The tempo and tension had increased a hundred fold. Everything else faded into a strange unreality.

The first of the progress reports showed that the daily schedule was being met. But Phil knew the time would inevitably come when something unforeseen would throw him behind. He wondered how Agren found the new pressure and, wanting to check on tie deliveries, Phil made the short walk to the sawmill.

The constant high whine of the saw, the crash and thunder of logs, the shouts of the workers and the line of the big wagons loading with finished ties, showed that Agren must be equally busy. Phil worked his way through the crowd on the platform and entered the office. Agren sat behind a littered desk, coat off, sleeves rolled up. He looked up and his eyes rounded then grew cold as his jaw hardened. He jumped up. "By God, I wouldn't think you'd show your face in here, Ward!"

Phil's jaw dropped. "Why shouldn't I, Hal?"

"You know damned well why! What did you try at Devil's Canyon?"

Phil stared, unbelieving. "What, Hal?"

"Riding alone with Carol! Trying to kiss her. I've heard about it!"

"From Carol?" Phil asked thinly.

"Of course not! But at least four people who were out there have told me about it. By God, I don't—"

Phil's voice cracked like a whip. "Somebody lied. Sure, I rode with Carol, showing her around. But if you're fool enough—"

Agren circled the desk, swung at Phil's head. Phil slipped under the blow, stepped in close and grabbed Agren's wrists, forcing his arms to his sides. Hal glared, eyes wild with anger.

"Hal! Listen to me!"

Agren wrenched free and slammed his fist at Phil's chin. Phil jerked his head to one side and the blow glanced off his cheek. He saw that it would be useless to talk to the man. Nor would Agren let him go without a fight. Still, he tried.

He shoved Agren to the desk, turned on his heel and took a couple of steps to the door. He heard Agren's rush and wheeled to meet the attack. He parried a wide swinging blow and then slammed his fist against an outthrust chin. Agren slammed back onto the desk top, scattering papers. He lay there, glassy-eyed.

Phil looked at him, fists slowly unclenching. "Hal, you started this. I tried to tell you the truth. Ask Carol. If you think she'd lie, you don't know the kind of woman you're getting." Agren slowly sat up, holding his jaw. Phil shrugged. "I'm willing to forget this happened, but maybe you want time to think it over. I'll be at my office or house any time."

He closed the door behind him. He worked his way through the crowd in the outer office, ignoring the stares of those who had heard the sound of the fight. He walked away from the sawmill, still angry. But now worry began to gnaw at him. He couldn't afford to make an enemy of Hal Agren. They must work too closely together, and cooperation could mean the difference between success or failure.

Back in the office, Agren arose from the desk. The door burst open and he glared at the clerk and cursed him out of the office. The door closed again and Agren felt along his jaw and winced. His face twisted in fury.

The thought flashed through his mind that maybe Ward was right—he should ask Carol. But too many had passed on the rumor of Devil's Canyon, and there was a ring of authenticity to the story. Agren's scowl darkened. By God, he ought to figure some way to ruin Ward! But this might lead to danger to himself. His anger slowly ebbed, though he still scowled. This fight was on good—and it could hurt Hal Agren. He should hunt up Ward, buy a drink and apologize—and cover his real feelings. Ask Carol? Why should he be such a fool! She'd evade or twist the thing around to make it look all right.

There was a quick pound of feet outside the office door and it burst open. Jensen, the camp foreman, showing the marks of a long, hard ride, strode to the desk. His face was drawn and grim. "Better get out to the camp. Hell's broke loose!"

Hal started up. "What's happened?"

"A bunch of gunslingers jumped the camp. Scattered the crew. Better hurry!"

Hal thought, in sudden fear, a camp destroyed! That would cut logging by half and he wouldn't be able to meet the rail contract. He grabbed his gunbelt with fumbling fingers, struggled into his coat.

He sent a clerk scurrying for half a dozen men with a reputation for fighting. In less than half an hour, the little cavalcade streamed out of town and raced along the forest trails. With each forward, pumping stride of his mount, Hal found his dread mounting. Fleming was right—you never knew what could happen!

He expected to find the camp in ashes, half the crew dead or wounded, the rest on their way to safer localities. Instead, when they burst into the clearing, they saw peaceful buildings, golden in the late afternoon sun. The workers were bunched near the cook shack. Hal saw no bandaged wounds or silent, sheet-covered forms. Hope lifted swiftly as he raced up and flung himself from the saddle.

He received a puzzling report. A bunch of renegade riders had suddenly appeared out of the woods and had come helling down on the camp, shooting and yelling. The crew took to its heels. The renegades caught a frightened Swede just outside the cook shack and they fired at his feet, making him dance, then chased him into the trees. They swaggered around and, as suddenly as they came, they rode off. Nothing touched or harmed, except half a dozen pies the cook had just baked. It didn't make sense.

Agren felt a deep wave of relief. He found a dozen explanations, most of them farfetched.

The foreman said, "Must have been that Lazy R bunch. Kind of looked like 'em."

Milt Reiger . . . Agren recalled the ambush near Devil's Canyon and the attempt to wreck the freight wagons. This camp, and the others in the woods, were close to the Lazy R as well as the Flying W. He had been too closely associated with Ward at Latigo, and later at Devil's Canyon and Ensign. If Reiger struck at him, he had probably also struck at Ward.

Hal paced around in jerky strides. Maybe it would be best for him to get back to Ensign and make clear that he and Ward were not partners—hardly even friends, now.

He realized he was being watched, and that this new fear must plainly show. He caught himself and squared his shoulders, smiled with a false confidence as he turned to the foreman. "We'll make sure this doesn't happen again. I'll leave the boys I brought, just in case they decide to visit us again."

The men seemed reassured, and returned to their jobs. Agren mounted his horse and headed back to town. He rode along the narrow forest road, thinking about Ward. He couldn't break with Phil, too much depended on it. They'd have to work together. Maybe there was some way Reiger could be made to understand. Word could be sent to the Lazy R, or maybe Hal would run into Reiger himself.

His horse suddenly snorted. Agren looked up and saw the black-clad, sinister figure of Dave Trego. The gunman sat his horse in the middle of the trail, right hand resting close to his holster, thin lips twisted in a mocking, triumphant smile. The mottled, deep-set eyes gleamed. "I've been waiting for this, Agren. Like I said, no man pulls a gun on me!"

Hal felt a new shock of fear. He saw deadly intent in the bony face and his eyes held on the hand so near the holster. Trego's flat voice pulled Hal's eyes back to the grim face again. "You're wearing a gun. Make your play."

Hal faced swift and certain death. His mouth went dry; his face grew clammy and he could not will himself to move. He could only stare at the gunman, face pale, speech paralyzed.

Trego waited eternal minutes and then rode forward, slowly. His eyes never left Hal's and his hand never moved far from his gun. Contempt replaced the grim expression and the lips curled as Trego came beside Hal. The flecked eyes bored deep.

Suddenly Trego's hand lifted and he brought it across Hal's face in a stinging slap. Hal rocked with the force of the blow and involuntarily cried out. He caught himself, sat immobile again, fingers white about the saddlehorn.

Trego considered the bulge of the holster and Colt under Hal's long coat. His voice was a lash. "You're a damn fraud, Agren. You wear a gun but you ain't got the guts to use it except behind a man's back. You ain't got the guts to face a fight— or to hold your girl."

Agren winced, but said nothing. He didn't dare or he'd get a bullet. Trego spat contemptuously. "A weak, rotten yellow-belly for all your loud talk. But maybe you'll do for the job."

"What job?" Agren's voice came out high and held a tremor.

Trego jerked open Hal's coat and lifted the Colt from its holster. He stuck the weapon under his own belt, reined around, motioned off the trail. "Get riding!"

Hal lifted the reins. "Where?" he choked.

"Lazy R. I don't know what the hell Milt wants with you, but he said bring you in. Come on! Move!"

Agren, a weak flood of relief sweeping over him, meekly urged his horse in the direction Trego indicated.

IX

Even though Ensign had doubled in size, news still travelled with amazing speed. Hal Agren had no more than left the sawmill with his picked men than a teamster waiting his load passed word of what he had overheard to a clerk. The clerk, who had the straight story from the head bookkeeper, corrected the teamster and three others listened as he told exactly what had happened. Five minutes later, one of the three wandered to a saloon on the main street. He told the story of the raid on the lumber camp.

The tale progressed steadily and within an hour Phil Ward looked up when the head clerk came up to his desk.

"I don't know if it's important to us," he said, "but you heard about Agren's bad luck?"

Phil dropped his pen. "What bad luck?"

He listened with growing concern as the man told the version he had heard. The clerk glanced at the clock on the wall. "Agren took a bunch of his boys and headed out there. I reckon the fight'll be over by now."

Phil thanked the man for the information and dismissed him. When the door closed behind the man, Phil again looked at the clock. He frowned, fingers tapping on the desk. Some of his anger at

101

Agren still remained, but he had an impulse to gather some men from the yard here and ride out to help. But the fight would be over by now, as the clerk had suggested.

Phil made a wry grimace. Agren was in trouble, and Phil had no doubt as to the source of it—the same hit-and-run raiding that Reiger had used in his attempts to wreck the wagons. Phil would bet his last dollar there'd be no proof of Reiger behind this new attack. But if the camp was wrecked, then Agren wouldn't get ties to the railroad. Where would that leave Phil?

Phil again glanced at the clock and reached for his gunbelt hanging on a rack nearby. It would be best if he rode out to the camp and offered to do all he could. His Flying W spread was not far away, and perhaps some of the crew could pitch in to rebuild if the damage was extensive. It would at least prove to Agren that Phil would not let personal disagreement block business cooperation.

He rode out of Ensign, taking a shorter road than Hal and his men had used. This would take Phil along the edge of the Flying W, near where it joined with Lazy R. He rode at a steady, ground-eating lope along the eastern fringe of the forest. To his right, he had several glimpses of his rolling range through the trees. Then the narrow trail angled away and plunged into the woods.

He kept to a steady lope, alert for the first

glimpse of the camp or any distant sound that might tell him a gun fight still continued. He passed a side trail with only a glance, increasing the horse's pace. Not ten minutes after he passed, Hal Agren rode out of the side trail, Dave Trego just behind him. Agren drew rein when they reached this wider way, but Trego waved him on.

"You keep riding," he snapped.

Agren's eyes flicked angrily, but he touched the horse with his spurs. Both men disappeared into the trees, angling off toward the Lazy R.

Phil followed the twists of the narrow road, eyes darting ahead into the strange half shadows of this forest light. It was a weird world under the trees, seemingly far from the familiar open ranges but a short distance away.

Suddenly he drew rein, hearing the low, steady rhythm of many horses coming toward him. He loosened his Colt and reined the horse off the trail. But he was not soon enough. As the horse brushed aside the low bushes, a dozen or more riders swept around the trail. Phil had a glimpse of harsh, hawklike faces beneath nondescript wide-brimmed hats, of a subdued glitter of cartridge-studded gunbelts. Then a shout rose and the lead rider pointed toward him.

"There goes another one!"

Phil thought they might be Agren's men, and his tightened rein halted the horse. They swept closer. Phil saw that they bore the marks of the hard trails. These were not loggers, temporarily mounted. He raked spurs in a slashing rowel and the horse plunged into the trees. A gun roared, and the bullet thudded into a thick trunk. Phil's hand dropped and he snapped a shot as a warning. The trees temporarily hid him.

He could hear the shouts of the riders on all sides. They streamed into the trees after him, spreading out to catch him in a noose of gunmen, with Phil in the center. For a time he raced to outdistance the men he could hear far on either side. He knew they tried to cut him off and then drive him back into the guns of the riders who crashed through the woods directly behind him.

Phil's pace planed down. This headlong rush to outdistance them was just what they expected. He tried to place the men by the sounds of the pursuit. Then his eyes sparked and suddenly he changed directions, bearing left and around.

He saw a fallen tangle of dead trees and brush, swung his horse around it, pulled it to a sliding halt. He vaulted from the saddle, grabbed the animal's muzzle with his left hand while his right held the Colt shoulder high, hammer dogged back.

The sound of pursuit grew louder, but he knew the patch of fallen timber would split the riders. His horse suddenly tossed its head, but Phil's strong fingers tightened on the muzzle and the animal stood still.

He heard the thud of hoofs just beyond the

windfall, heard the excited calls of the men. They swept around the tangle, swinging wide. He had a glimpse through the distant trees of riders flashing by, and he heard them a short distance behind. Had any of them turned his head, Phil would have been discovered. He stood taut and still, listening to the fading sounds. He released the horse, holstered the gun and swung into the saddle. He placed his position and then set the horse at a fast trot through the trees, angling back to the trail. Now and then he looked back. Once he reined in to listen but the forest silence was unbroken. He smiled in grim triumph and rode on. Somewhere a dozen puzzled rides scoured the woods and wondered how their quarry had escaped.

He reached the lumber camp an hour later. The foreman told him what had happened. Phil looked around, knowing now that the raiders had made a huge swing through the woods and had circled back toward the open range. He had just happened to meet up with them. He was pleased to learn that no damage had been done and that the flow of rail ties would be uninterrupted. He asked about Agren and the foreman told him Hal had returned to Ensign. Phil considered going on to the Flying W, but there was too much work waiting for him. Regretfully, he set himself to the long ride back.

He set an easy pace. He thought of the raiders

and his eyes grew bleak. They had the vulture look of the renegades who worked for the Lazy R. Reiger again. Sooner or later, Phil promised himself, there'd come a time when Reiger would slip. Then the law—or Phil—could move in on him.

It was late in the afternoon when Hal Agren rode into the huge, littered yard of the Lazy R. He saw men milling in the corral, unsaddling horses that showed the dust and sweat streaks of hard riding. Agren saw Milt Reiger near the corral gate, listening to one of the men, who pointed toward the timber land. Agren caught a few words.

". . . slipped us somehow. But he won't ride so free and easy after this. We could—"

"Climb down," Trego's brief order cut in. Reiger looked around and his heavy face lighted. He strode up as Agren swung out of the saddle and faced him. Reiger's smile tried to be friendly. "Welcome to Lazy R."

Agren glared. "A hell of a welcome!"

Reiger shrugged. "It was the only way we could get you here. Come inside."

Agren found enough courage to balk. "Now wait a minute! I'd like to know why my camp was raided and why I'm brought here at gunpoint."

A touch of steel came in Reiger's voice. "We'll talk about it inside."

He strode toward the ranch house. Agren

glanced at Trego, who coldly made a slight motion to follow the rancher. Agren reluctantly obeyed.

The main room of the house, like the yard, was spacious and cluttered. The furniture was crude, with marks of hard and careless wear. Glass and bottle rings mottled the table top, and every chair rung showed the scars of spurs. The floor had been only casually swept so that there was a ring of dust and grime about the room.

Reiger sailed his hat onto a sagging sofa in a far corner, picked bottle and glasses from a sideboard and brought them to the table. He kicked up chairs. "Rest your feet, Agren, and have a drink. We got talking to do."

Agren looked around. Trego now stood beside the closed door, leaning against the wall. His planed, bony face and sunken eyes showed no expression but Agren felt the continued, silent threat of the black-clad figure. He looked again at Reiger.

The rancher gestured toward the chair. "Sit down, man! Take a drink—you need it. You can figure later whether you're among friends or not."

"Friends!" Agren exploded and gestured toward the corral. "Those riders raided my camp. They're your crew! And you talk about friends!"

Trego came forward like a black shadow. "Why don't you have your drink and listen? It'll save time and trouble."

Agren caught the edge of menace. He slowly sat down, reached for the glass of whisky. Reiger smiled and sat down in his own chair. Trego completed the trio about the table.

"To us." Reiger lifted his glass. Agren hesitated and then drank. Reiger studied him. "How good a friend do you figure Phil Ward is?"

Agren shot a quick glance at Trego, back at Reiger, tried to determine where this question would lead. He felt he must play it close. "Friend?" he said slowly. "What has he to do with bringing me here?"

Reiger said slowly, "That's no answer."

Agren fingered the glass. "Phil's easy to work with." He sought for words. "We keep in touch with one another because of the railroad contracts. Our equipment happened to be shipped together. Maybe you'd call him a business friend."

Reiger's thick brow lifted and he glanced at Trego. "I reckon we had it wrong then. We thought you were real close. That's why we couldn't figure what he was doing with your woman at Devil's Canyon."

Agren froze and caution left him. "With Carol?"

"With her," Reiger answered. "Dave and me happened to see Ward and her out there in the woods. I'd heard that you were courting her, and I couldn't quite figure what she was doing with him."

Agren checked the lift of jealousy, feeling these

two wanted to spur him because of it. His tone held a false, light note. "I can explain that. Her brother had to look over the camp and she went along. Phil showed her around."

Trego laughed, a contemptuous sound that raked across Agren like a knife. "Ward wasn't showing her much scenery. He was doing a big job of sweet-talking, and she was listening real close."

Agren's fist slammed on the table. "That's a lie! Carol wouldn't—" He broke off, mouth hanging open in sudden fear of the slitted, angry eyes of the gunhawk.

Reiger spoke smoothly. "Pay no attention, Dave. Agren didn't mean it. How'd *you* feel if you learned your friend was trying to steal your girl? Just forget it."

Agren's eyes moved from one to the other. Reiger had an expression of pitying concern that was galling. Trego pursed his thin lips and eased back in his chair. Neither said a word, and it was more damning than if they had tried to convince him. He gathered that they didn't have to. They knew.

Agren moistened his lips. "You're sure?"

Reiger lifted his heavy shoulders in a shrug. "Dave and me saw 'em. Ward kissed her several times—that's why we couldn't figure how he could be a real friend of yours."

Agren's chest felt tight and there was a twist of

angry nerves in the pit of his stomach. This confirmed the talk he had heard in town. Seething jealousy choked him, and he had to get away from the painful subject. His anger fastened on Trego's high-handed action but it was partially checked by the silent, deadly threat of the gunman. "I was brought here so you could tell me this!"

"Part of the reason," Reiger nodded.

Agren leaned forward, eyes glittering. "You're such a damn good friend! Why the raid on my camp?"

Reiger grinned. "Wasn't anybody hurt, was there? Did you see any damage? The boys had orders just to hooraw the place." His face set, granitelike, around the mouth. "Get this straight, Agren. If we'd wanted to tear up your camp, there wouldn't be a thing left standing and you'd have no crew. It was a sure way to get you up here." Agren glared as Reiger's jaw jutted out. "If there is a next time, you won't have a camp, Agren."

Agren looked from Reiger's harsh face to Trego's skull-like features. "Next time?" he asked, voice suddenly dry.

Reiger smiled again and refilled Agren's glass. "I don't figure there will be. You're smart as they come. I've been watching you. I want to make a deal."

"Deal? With me?"

Reiger leaned forward. "Yeah, now that we've

told you about Ward and your girl and what he'll do if he has the chance. He'll do the same thing in business. I got reason to hate Ward, too. So the deal's simple. Help me ruin Phil Ward—break him! We'll run him out of the country if he ain't killed first."

Agren's jaw dropped and Reiger saw the flicker of uncertainty and fear back in his eyes. The big man lowered his bullet head between his massive shoulders. "That ain't much of a deal, as it stands. But there's more—plenty more for you and me. If we can make Ward default on his railroad contracts, we both stand to profit."

"How?" Agren blurted.

Reiger's interlaced fingers relaxed. He had his man now. He made a sweeping gesture. "Western Pacific is going to build a railroad, no matter who goes under. So if Ward can't grade and lay steel, or furnish beef, the railroad will give those contracts to someone else." He stabbed a blunt finger across the table at Agren. "You take the grading work. I want the beef contract . . . and Ward's ranch."

Agren sat fascinated. He looked at Trego as though to read even more in the impassive face. He looked back at Reiger. "Me—take the grading? I don't have the equipment or the men."

Reiger laughed. "I don't have Flying W, either. But you forget the penalties. If Ward can't meet the contracts, he'll go bankrupt. You'll pick up everything for a penny on the dollar or less. His construction crew is already at work—they just swing over to your payroll. You got two contracts, and you're making more money'n you've ever seen before."

Agren's mind fastened on that and the thought of Phil Ward no longer near Carol. He wet his lips and started to shake his head, but Reiger's lifted palm checked him.

"Don't worry about trouble. Dave can take care of any gunslinging and I got a crew that ain't afraid of a little fighting. I'll handle that end of it and maybe see some Flying W beef disappear. You know business so I figure you could throw a little money into a deal like this." Reiger leaned back. "There it is. That's why we faked a raid on the camp to bring you up here."

He waited and Trego sat impassive, hooded green eyes covertly watching Agren. Hal hastily took another drink, his mind racing. It made sense, and he'd certainly stand to come out far ahead on the deal. Still he hesitated; Phil trusted him.

Unconsciously his lips curled. Maybe Ward took advantage of that trust with Carol. Revulsion at the trend of his thoughts made him grimace, and Reiger caught the expression. He shot a sidelong glance at Trego.

Agren pressed his lips so tightly his cheeks puffed and he shook his head. "You wasted your time, Reiger. I can't do it."

Reiger's thick fingers beat an impatient tattoo on the table. Trego stirred and Agren's eyes instantly shot to him and away again.

"Wasted my time?" Reiger repeated. "Maybe . . . maybe not. Ward ain't done you a bit of good, Agren. Not a bit."

"He's helped," Agren said, sullenness in his voice.

"Has he?" Reiger grunted. "There's just the three of us, so we can talk straight. Nothing said here but Dave and me wouldn't deny." He again pointed his finger at Agren. "He's helped you, huh? How about the time you was shot at on the way back from Latigo? How about the time you come near losing your equipment over the rim of Devil's Canyon? If you hadn't been with him, you'd never had those risks."

"You're admitting you did that!" Agren exclaimed.

"Just talking about 'em, and maybe thinking what might happen if things don't change. For instance, this raid on your timber camp. It could happen again tomorrow." His voice dropped. "For real."

Agren stared in growing fear.

Reiger's heavy voice bore down on him. "Lots of places a bushwhacker could lay up in the woods, and you always have to ride 'em, Agren. There's logs, shavings and sawdust around your sawmill. It could go up in smoke some night . . . spontaneous combustion, maybe."

"You'd do that!" The words dragged out of Agren's throat.

"Why, man, you never can tell what'll happen! Life is full of chances." Reiger's broad face grew mean as he jerked his thumb toward the black-clad gunman. "Another thing, you put a gun on Dave. I've kept him from settling that tally. I'm running out of patience, though, unless you're smart. If you ain't, why should I worry about Dave's personal scores?"

Agren swallowed. Reiger drove in the final point. "You let Ward go on as he has behind your back, and you'll wind up with no girl. Dave and me know what we saw." He made a wide gesture. "You're not blind, Agren; you're not a fool. You see how it stacks up. You stand to win a hell of a lot of money and keep your girl—or you can lose everything quick, and maybe your life with the rest of it. Decide!"

The deadly, strained silence descended. Agren felt that Trego, though he hadn't moved a muscle, stood poised like a ferocious dog on a thin leash. He'd never have a chance against that gun, nor against the ambushers that Reiger hinted might also wait.

Agren swallowed. "All right. I'll throw in. You get the beef contract. I get the construction job."

Reiger's coarse face broke into a wide grin and his hand smashed onto the table. He reached for the bottle. "By God! I knew you'd see it! Have a drink—a big one! We got plans to make and talking to do . . . partner!"

Agren accepted the glass and lifted it. "Partner." It didn't come easy, not with this man.

Then he thought of Ward kissing Carol, scheming to take her from him. Agren's glass lifted higher and he downed the drink.

X

Phil felt that the work progressed slowly, especially during the period when ballast and rails were first delivered across the trestle. Scrapers and graders seemed to shape the road-bed much too slowly and to watch a man with a shovel was like watching an ant gnawing at a mountain. But everyone seemed satisfied and Phil decided that his impatience stemmed from his unfamiliarity with the job. He could not stay long at the camp but had to ride to Ensign.

When he returned to the construction camp, he was amazed at the amount of track that had been built. It now extended from the trestle westward to the forest, two bright lines of steel that would bring the swift pace of commerce to this district.

He rode to the end-of-track with Tim Moriarty on a work train, the flats loaded with rail and ballast. Swinging down from one of the flats, Phil and the big Irishman walked ahead of the train.

Dust clouds arose as scrapers and graders worked; men swore luridly at teams, and choked on the dust. Phil began to feel a sense of having a part in something big and important. People, wealth, goods would come and go along these rails because of Phil Ward. Tim had been watching him and the big man's eyes deepened in understanding and then sparkled.

"Would ye be catching the fever of railroad building, me bucko?"

Phil caught himself and laughed. "I'll tell you how I feel when this is finished. But if it keeps up as smoothly as it has, I just might take it on to the Pacific."

"*Whsst,* now! It's big talk you're making! The time for troubles has not yet come, but 'twill be upon us. That ye can depend on!"

"Maybe," Phil said. "I hope you're wrong."

"Ah, 'tis good to see the iron jump forward," Tim said soberly.

"A mile a day, according to reports," Phil said complacently.

"That it is. But have ye ever noticed that it always goes best just before the devil uses his hoof?"

Phil chuckled. "No sign of the devil here yet, Tim."

"Ah, but ye must never disregard the black spalpeen."

Phil returned to Ensign the next day, Tim going with him to make sure of the payroll. Two days later, Hedgren, the local freighting manager, sent over two Wells Fargo strong boxes. The payroll was made up and reloaded in the boxes. The following day, innocent freight wagons lumbered out to the camp where the superintendent paid the men.

Each day Phil read the construction reports. They still showed that the work progressed without a hitch and, actually, each day saw just a tiny fraction of the work done ahead of schedule. Phil kept Tim's warning in mind, but as the days passed, the memory of it dulled more and more, nor did Tim bring up the subject again.

He often saw Hal Agren, but only during business hours. Agren's ties arrived like clockwork at the end-of-track where they were stacked immediately behind the graders. But the big piles melted as they were strung out like black bars along the roadbed.

Agren seemed to have changed and Phil began to hope that he no longer had a motive for jealousy. The greater part of the time, Phil was away from Ensign. Carol obviously preferred Agren and there was no point in letting some important problem go unsolved on the long chance that he might get a few moments with her. And probably not alone, for Agren had really embarked upon a campaign to win the girl.

Fleming himself confirmed it one day when Phil went to his office to make a requisition for supplies. Fleming signed the forms and then leaned back in his chair, in a mood to relax.

"You're doing a good job, Phil. But you're working too hard. It shows."

Phil shrugged. "We have to keep things moving. Otherwise you'd be raising hell."

Fleming smiled. "That's right, but I don't like to send my contractors to boothill. Take a few days off up at your ranch."

"I'd be checking the beef," Phil said wryly.

"Then here in town. Play poker and lose a few dollars. I think we could manage to have you to dinner a couple of times."

Phil wanted to accept. The last few weeks had been filled with driving days, a million problems, a constant pressure. It would be good to see Carol again, but Phil hesitated.

"Carol will be busy, Ray."

Fleming looked thoughtfully out the window. "Hal takes a good deal of her time." He threw Phil a covert glance. "I had the idea in the beginning that you'd be around as much as Hal."

Phil was startled, but quickly masked it. "When would I have the time?"

Fleming nodded, although he didn't quite accept this as a full explanation. "I know how that can be. Used to keep me pushing and driving until I was exhausted. Now I know better. This job can kill you if you let it."

"It will be over when the rails reach the Colorado," Phil said.

"That's why you shouldn't push so hard." He hesitated and gave Phil a sidelong look. "Sometimes a man can give attention to one thing while something of far more value gets by him."

Phil sighed and rose. "Each of us has his problems, Ray. Mine's the railroad until the contract's completed."

"I suppose so," Fleming sighed. "Keep building."

"I will."

Things continued well until the end of the week. The work reports no longer showed a slight gain but they were still within the limits set by the railroad. Phil didn't worry about it, but Tim was faintly troubled.

"Sure, we're doing fine," he agreed. "But the foremen know the further you're ahead, the more leeway ye have when trouble comes."

"You've picked a good crew, Tim, and good foremen. I'm not worried."

Phil had to go out to the ranch and then to Agren's camps. He was gone for four days. When he returned, Tim shoved reports at him without a word. Phil studied them, looked up at Tim.

"Behind schedule, and increasing every day."

"Don't I know it!" the Irishman grumbled. "There has been no complaint from the camp, but I know there will be. Something is out of hand there."

"Why hasn't the superintendent reported it?" Phil demanded.

Tim snorted. "Now would you if there was a chance you could whip it? Sure, ye'd try to clean up the trouble yourself."

Phil dropped the papers on the desk. "Then what should we do? I'm for letting the superintendent whip it his own way."

"That may be best," Tim agreed. "Give him two more days."

The morning of the third day, Tim pushed more reports at Phil, his moon face dark and frowning.

"The work falls off more and more. 'Tis time you and me looked for ourselves, and the sooner the better."

Phil read the reports. Roadbed graded, ties placed and track laid had dropped considerably. Copies of this report would go to Fleming, and the engineers would be coming around to find out what was happening. Phil dropped the reports on the desk.

"We'll leave this afternoon," he said.

He half expected to see Fleming, but he and Tim saddled horses and rode out without having a glimpse of the engineer. They arrived at the camp after dark and the lights from the saloon district were brighter than ever. In the area of the bunkhouses there was little foot traffic. Kitchen laborers cleaned up the debris from the camp supper, not long finished. There was little indication of any serious trouble.

They rode to the superintendent's quarters. Phil immediately brought up the matter of the slipping work schedule, and the superintendent sighed.

"I was going to make a personal report in a day

or two. I thought I could get it straightened out."

"I understand," Phil nodded. "But what is happening?"

"Something makes this bunch as bad as I've ever seen. Every night is pay night, the way they guzzle rotgut."

"Lost time," Tim grunted.

The superintendent nodded. "Too many of them staying in their bunks recovering from drunken brawls. We have constant calls to patch up knife cuts or badly beaten men. This is getting out of hand. I've jumped on the foreman to get this situation under control."

"That didn't help?" Phil asked.

"Not so you could notice it. The men are surly. They lean too long on their shovels. They act as if they want nothing more than a hell of a good fight with the foremen and bosses."

Tim growled angrily, "Now that don't make sense."

"I think one of the saloons is putting out free rotgut."

"You've questioned the men?"

"None of 'em will talk. They're afraid the free liquor will stop if they do. I think that along with the fire water, they're being told that they're working too hard. They're all slowing down."

The Irishman's face reflected surprise. "It doesn't make sense. I never heard of a saloon-keeper eager to give his booze away."

"Maybe he isn't," Phil said slowly. Tim's eyes widened.

"Ye'd be thinking someone else is paying him—"

"To stop the railroad, or us."

Tim shook his head. "Now that's a hell of a roundabout way to be doing it. Why not use dynamite, or maybe fire the camp?"

"They'd risk jail, or a bullet. You can't arrest a man for giving away his stock. You can't arrest a man for paying for drinks for others. What do you do?"

"In the meantime, we drop behind schedule," the superintendent said.

"And the penalty clauses will start," Phil completed the thought. "We'll have everything going out and nothing coming in." He abruptly arose. "Tim, we'd better take a good look around right now."

"Make sure your Colt is ready for use," Tim said grimly. "It's bad trouble we could be having."

They left the superintendent's quarters and strode up the street. As they approached the tent town the noise increased in a steady roar. They came out onto the single main street of the district. Light and noise beat at them like physical things. The dusty street was filled with milling men who wandered from saloon to saloon or pushed their way into the dancehalls and gambling hells.

Phil and Tim were jostled constantly. Before,

each tent, barkers shouted brazenly. Phil pulled Tim into the comparative quiet of a passageway between two buildings. From one side came the steady beat of a tinny piano and the shuffling pound of boots dancing clumsily on the wooden floor. A woman's shrill, harsh laughter came to them. From the other tent wall came the sound of faro dealers and chuck-a-luck men calling the turns of fortune.

"Does this go on every night?" Phil demanded.

"Always has," Tim frowned worriedly. "But this is the middle of the week and those spalpeens should've been dead broke long since."

"No one's financing all that." Phil indicated the crowded street.

"Have ye noticed that most of them are just drunk? Actually the hell holes are doing little business."

"Let's find out where they get it," Phil said shortly and walked out on the street again. They went to several saloons and in each the men seemed to be paying for their drinks. In half an hour Phil and Tim stood out on the street as puzzled as ever.

"We just haven't found the right one yet," Phil said stubbornly.

He started across a narrow alley that gave on a row of cribhouses, Tim following him. One of the small shacks erupted two fighting men. A woman screamed loudly. Phil stopped short. The doors of the other shacks swung open. Suddenly a voice sounded, loud and jubilant, behind Phil.

"A fight! Come on, bucko-boys!"

A rush swept Phil into the alley. He heard someone yell defiantly and then he found himself in the midst of brawling, fighting men. It was pandemonium. A burly man's fist clipped along his ear, knocking him to one side. Powerful arms circled him and contracted into a tightening band. A whisky breath fanned his face.

Phil kicked back viciously. The man howled and the arms fell loose. Phil pivoted and his fist lashed into a heavy, drunken face. The man's head snapped back and he fell into the crowd. Another hand grabbed Phil's shoulder.

Phil twisted free, barely avoiding a maul like fist that would have smashed his nose across his face had it landed. He heard a crash of wood as a mass of brawling men slammed into one of the flimsy crib houses. Women's yells and screams punctuated the shouting, cursing wave of noise that beat between the walls.

This was a riot. Phil took a quick bearing and then grimly fought his way out of the pack. There was always some drunken, blood lusting worker ready to throw a fist or a vicious, treacherous kick.

At last Phil broke free. His hat was gone and there was a trickle of blood from the corner a his mouth. He spat out the salty taste and moved away to catch his breath. The fight raged up and down the alley and he wondered how many men would be crippled, how much the work schedule would fall behind in the next day.

Tim appeared at the edge of the crowd. Three men clung to him, but Tim shook them loose. His fist sent one man tumbling headlong and his thick arm sent a second staggering back. The third suddenly ran. Tim's shirt was ripped down the front and his hat was gone.

He came striding to Phil, moon face alight, his hands clenched into sledge-hammer fists. The muscles of one arm bunched like writhing snakes where the shirt sleeve had been torn away. He grinned and swiped the back of his hand across his face.

"Sure and 'tis like a Kilkenny fair. It brings a lift to me heart to see much a brawl!"

"They'll wreck the whole place," Phil snapped.

Tim glanced around.

"Sure, and the camp would be peaceful and we'd have a chance of building road again."

"I think that's the answer, Tim. Let's get out of here." For all his anger and worry, Phil could not help grinning at him. "There's enough Mick in you to enjoy a good fight."

Tim looked offended and then grinned widely. "And would ye deny an Irishman a bit of a brawl?"

"I hope you made the most of it," Phil said

grimly. Tim looked puzzled, but Phil said no more. . . .

The next morning Phil read work reports. There were many absences because of injuries received in the fight. Phil had hoped the tent town would be destroyed but the area stood undisturbed and peaceful. He read the reports with mounting anger, and finally looked up at Tim.

"Let's go to the hospital."

Phil talked forcefully to the doctor in charge, who brought in a man whose cheek was bandaged and whose eyes looked watery and sick.

"Salton Arnold," the doctor said, glancing at a card record. "Admitted for a knife wound. Also drunk."

Arnold looked fearfully at the doctor, Tim and Phil. His knees buckled, face green with nausea. Phil stepped to him, grabbed the frowzled hair and jerked the man's head up:

"Who gave you the drinks?"

Arnold's eyes gradually focused. He dredged up a last bit of defiance. His weak lips managed to curl and he spoke in a rasping whisper.

"I bought my own."

"You're lying," Phil said. "You had less than a dollar on you when you were brought in. You'll tell the truth, or you'll stay in jail until you rot."

Arnold's sick eyes cast around the circle of grim faces and his defiance left him, like the air out of a cheap balloon.

"Pennard's place," he whispered. "But don't let him know I told you. He'd send that gundog of his after me. Braxton ain't a man to fool around with."

"Pennard," the doctor said. "He's a newcomer to tent town. A lot of fights start there."

"Why does he give you the whisky?" Phil demanded.

"He's always standing the boys for a drink. He says he don't like to see us sweating our guts out on the railroad for so little pay."

Phil looked at him in amazement. "A saloon-keeper says that!"

"Pennard says other railroad contractors pay a hell of a lot better than this job. We should either quit or work less to even the score. He's mighty free with his liquor."

Phil stepped back and the doctor led Arnold out of the office. Phil stared at the far wall, unseeing, puzzled. Tim stirred restlessly.

"It doesn't make sense. I know Pennard; he ain't filled with sweetness and light."

Phil looked up. "It doesn't make sense unless someone wants to wreck us. I'm going to talk to Mr. Pennard."

Tim immediately arose. "It's a long time since I was in his High Iron."

"I'll go alone, Tim," Phil said. Tim started to argue but Phil cut him short. "Mr. Pennard will probably talk more freely if I'm alone."

"Or slit your throat," Tim growled.

"Hardly that, Tim. He'd know he'd hang."

Despite Tim's protests, Phil went into tent town alone. The street was nearly empty and all the tent places looked tawdry and deserted. As Phil walked down the street, he was eyed by an occasional swamper who made lazy and ineffectual efforts to clean up the litter in front of each establishment.

At Pennard's High Iron, a man wearing belt and holstered gun lounged beside the door yawning into the street. Phil halted a few feet away.

"Where can I find Pennard?"

The gunhawk studied him, narrow face insolent. He removed a toothpick from his thin lips and gestured to the door.

"His office is in the back. Be sure you knock."

"I'll remember," Phil said scornfully and walked into the tent.

The gunman entered behind him, but Phil disregarded him. He strode across the huge main area. There was a repulsive smell of ancient tobacco, cheap whisky and sweat about the place. Phil walked toward a wood partition and a closed door marked "Office."

He turned the knob and entered, hardly breaking his stride. Facing the door was a large table that served as a desk and Pennard sat behind it, his eyes filled with a weary evil.

"Don't you ever knock?"

"Not here," Phil said shortly.

"We could teach him manners," a harsh voice said, and Phil then saw the man who stood to one side. He was tall, broad, with a deep chest and a paunch that hung over the cartridge-filled belt. His holster rode slightly high on his right leg so that the Colt's butt came exactly between his elbow and wrist. Here was a real gunman, Phil thought. A glance at the heavy, cruel face with the cold eyes confirmed it.

"Maybe later, Braxton," Pennard said.

Phil heard the first gunman step into the office behind him but he did not turn his head. Pennard smiled. "What can I do for you?"

"Why are you giving rotgut to my men? Why are you making them slow up with the work?"

"Am I?" Pennard asked carelessly. "Who says so?"

"You haven't answered my questions."

"I don't intend to," Pennard snapped. "What I do is my own business."

"You've made it mine. I've had enough of this end-of-track scum, Pennard."

Pennard chuckled. "Now that's too damn bad, Ward. What do you intend to do about it?"

"Close it up—every damn bordello and saloon."

Braxton stirred and Pennard's grin grew wider. He sucked at his lips so that hollows appeared in his sallow cheeks.

"A mighty big job, Ward. Now where would you start?"

"I could start here."

"You could—but you won't." His smile widened. He turned his hand on edge and his thumb lifted. Too late Phil realized this was a signal. Braxton moved suddenly and Phil wheeled about to face the gundog. He no more than glimpsed Braxton's outthrust jaw. Something crashed down on his head. The room whirled about in a sudden blaze of lights. The walls leaned in and the floor heaved upward.

Phil realized he was falling and then he realized nothing at all.

XI

Something bothered him and Phil tried to escape from it. He did not know that he opened his eyes but suddenly he became aware of a window and harsh, irritating sun. He moved again and his body became a mass of pain in his side, legs, arms and back. He remembered Pennard behind the desk, Braxton and the other gunhawk. Phil frowned, puzzled. He lay on a bed in a small room, the walls broken by a closed door and by the window through which the painful light streamed. He heard movement beside him and then a large hand lightly touched his own lying on the sheet that covered him.

"*Whsst!* Now would ye finally be stirring yourself!" Tim Moriarty's voice demanded. "It's high time ye took an interest in this world instead of the other."

Phil turned his head. Tim had evidently been sitting on the chair beside the bed but now he stood up, moon face beaming down on Phil. There was a faint discoloration under one eye.

"You've been fighting," Phil said. He was surprised at the weakness of his voice.

"Sure, listen to the bucko! I've been fighting! And what is it that put you here, I'd be asking?"

Phil frowned. "Where am I?"

"The camp hospital."

"Hospital!" Phil half rose, but a crushing wave of pain flattened him on the bed again, leaving him weak and sweating. Tim's concerned face came into focus again.

"Ye'll not be trying that again, me boy." Tim moved the chair and sat down where Phil could see him. Once again the light touched the mouse under his eye.

"How'd I get here?" Phil asked.

"Ye were found in an alley. Ye had some ribs cracked and blacksmiths had tried to shape your face into something else. Ye had a concussion that had us all worried until this very minute."

Phil was silent. Pennard's gunhawks and bully boys had done a good job on him. He admitted he had learned the hard way that being the big boss of the work camp had meant nothing to the scum of end-of-track. This would not be the end of it.

"How long have I been here?" he asked finally.

"A week."

"A week!" Phil gasped.

"It was not sure whether ye'd build railroad or play on a harp—assuming ye'd landed in the right place."

Phil noticed Tim's bruise again, "It looks as though you had a fight of your own."

Tim smiled fleetingly. "That I did. There was an argument. I won, but there is always someone who gets in a punch or two before they have the sense to give up."

"What was it about, Tim?"

Tim hesitated. Finally he lifted his massive shoulders in a shrug. "The men are getting badly out of hand. The word spread that ye'd been found, drunk and mauled."

"So?" Phil asked sharply.

"So the boss himself hits the rotgut and he is not bucko enough to ramrod a tough construction crew. It was a mistake that I had to correct."

"They working again?"

"They're working," Tim said and quickly left the room. He returned with the camp doctor, who was relieved to see that Phil had returned to consciousness.

"You've had a rough time of it. You've got to rest and mend."

"But—"

"But nothing!" the doctor snapped. "Tim and the superintendent can take care of the track well enough until you're back on the job. But you have to take it easy. That's orders. Out of the room, Tim, and let the man get some sleep."

"Sleep!" Phil said sarcastically.

The doctor had his way and there was nothing Phil could do but lie in bed and look out the window. He knew that there must be serious trouble in the camp or Tim Moriarty would not have been in a fight. Phil tried to dismiss the problem and to get the rest that the doctor prescribed. But he soon found that he considered a hundred and one problems of the camp and of the ranch. This was but a foretaste of what was to come. Each morning Tim would pay a brief visit and assure him that the work went on. But Phil knew the man did not tell the whole truth. It showed in restlessness and anger that the big Irishman could not wholly conceal. The fact that Tim spent most of his time in the construction camp was in itself an indication that all was not clear sailing.

Often, lying in bed during the long, dragging hours, Phil tried to evaluate himself and Carol. He knew that he was in love with her, but he also knew that she was not in love with him. He could not push himself at anyone, and where Phil had hesitated, Agren had pushed ahead. But Phil, painfully considering all these factors, could not quite give up the fight altogether. Somehow, some way, he would give Hal Agren a run for his money.

Phil was finally allowed to get up. He moved slowly about the room, walking awkwardly, favoring the heavily taped ribs, feeling the pull and strain of every bruised muscle. He swore that Joe Pennard and his gun-slammers would soon pay for this.

The next day, late in the afternoon, Phil sat resting in a chair. A knock sounded, the door opened, and Fleming stepped in. With a pleased exclamation, Phil jumped up. An iron talon gripped his side and he sank back, grimacing in pain.

"Hey!" Fleming eased Phil back into the chair. "You'd better move easy."

Phil managed a grin. "That's become a habit. It's good to see you."

Fleming sat down on the edge of the bed and considered Phil, judging his condition. "We heard about you back in town. Exactly what happened?"

Phil told about Pennard and Braxton and how he had later been found. "So here I am," he finished, "sadder and wiser. What did you hear in town?"

Fleming flushed. "You know how things get twisted. Some said you had yourself a fling at end-of-track, were given a mickey and rolled. Others say you got in a drunken brawl and came out at the short end."

Phil frowned. "What does Carol think?"

"Nothing—I guess."

"Let me have it," Phil said.

"She heard the story of the drunken fight. Hal Agren had it from someone. He didn't want to talk about it, but Carol insisted."

Phil could not picture Agren reluctant to talk about a thing like that. He rubbed his hand worriedly along his jaw.

"You know the truth, Ray. Tim Moriarty can confirm it. I don't know how the other story—"

"Forget it. I'll tell Carol what happened."

"You have to, Ray. I won't have her believing this of me."

"It will work out. You have far more important problems than my sister's opinion, Phil."

"That's hard to believe." Phil braced himself. "Let's have it, Ray."

"Well . . . work has slowed down. The daily reports show increasingly less progress, and it has me worried."

"The men are quitting?"

"No. They lean longer on their shovels, take longer to light their pipes, pass the time of day and consider the weather."

"So that's what's worrying Tim!" Phil said softly.

"It is. They simply can't get the steam up again. Something's wrong with the men." He pulled at his lower lip, frowning, more troubled than Phil had even seen him. At last he dropped his hand. "Slow-ups can be dangerous and costly, Phil. Tim's doing his best, but it's not enough. Each day the work falls farther and farther behind."

"Badly?"

Fleming made an eloquent gesture. "Grading and track laying is far behind. Hal has been sending ties at the old schedule and they're piling up unused."

"Is it worrying Hal?" Phil asked.

"There's no reason it should. He's fulfilling his

quota. How can he be penalized because your work is falling behind? Something else, Phil—it's tying up the work trains."

Phil looked sardonically at the engineer. "It's a cheerful report."

"I can't help it, Phil. We've scheduled in ballast and rails but we're piling up that material just as Hal piles up ties."

"What can I do?"

Fleming slapped his hat against the calf of his boot. He looked around the room. "How much longer will you be here?"

"I'd have been out days ago if I'd had my way. I can get around after a fashion, enough to get hold of things, maybe."

"Well," Fleming scratched his head, "don't rush it, of course. But the faster you're on the job the better."

"Then it's not all shot to pieces?"

"No, I can say that at least." Fleming walked to the door. "But it's not far from it, Phil. You're going to have a hard time catching up."

After Fleming left, Phil sat for a long time thinking over the situation. He tried to find some solution and realized that he had to know much more. He slowly pulled himself from the chair and called an attendant. He gave orders to send for Tim Moriarty and brushed aside the attendant's protest that he should be resting. . . .

Phil forced himself to wait patiently for Tim to

appear. It was late afternoon before Tim walked in. Phil motioned to the bed. "Sit down, Tim. . . . How bad is it?"

Tim pulled out a soiled bandana and mopped the sweat from his face. "Now what would make ye think that it's bad?"

"Rayburn Fleming was here. Let's have it as it stands."

"All right, ye'll have it. Understand that ye'd been told before but I thought it best ye not worry while you were getting well. I'll say we're still making roadbed and laying track, but that's all." He went on to tell of loafing, discontent, much fighting and little work. They were falling rapidly behind. "It's the end-of-track scum." Tim grimaced. "Joe Pennard and others of his kind. And there is little that can be done about it."

Phil moved restlessly in his chair; his fists clenched on its arms and his face grew grim. This was the first time he had seen Tim Moriarty looked discouraged. Phil's lips pressed tighter.

"I'm not so sure something can't be done about it, Tim. Get back on the job and do the best you can."

Tim nodded. "Fleming and me had talked just yesterday. I told him how things were and I put me best blarney into persuading him to give us an extension of time."

"He granted it?" Phil asked hopefully.

"It is not his to say, ye understand. He is but

the chief engineer and a thing like this must be decided back in the East. Fleming says they're likely to think it best to get a new contractor should ye fail, or to invoke the money penalties so that ye'll have to quit and make way for a man able to finish the job."

"From their viewpoint, that makes sense." Phil nodded. His face cleared. "Well, it's none of your worry, Tim, but mine. On your way out, send that doctor in here."

Tim left. Three days later Phil stepped carefully out of the hospital and walked to the light surrey Tim had driven up. He winced slightly as he slowly climbed to a seat. The Irishman looked hard at him, his blue eyes clouded.

"Ye're sure it's best ye leave the place?"

"I persuaded the doctor," Phil said shortly through set teeth. Tim nodded.

"Why should Tim Moriarty question any luck that comes his way? 'Tis little there's been the last week."

They wheeled down the street in a cloud of dust and Tim headed for Devil's Canyon. Phil looked surprised but said nothing. Phil saw the long trestle now spanning the canyon. But this side of it, spur lines had been laid and on each stood long strings of cars holding ballast and rails. Phil soundlessly whistled.

"All that's waiting for us?"

"All of that," Tim repeated grimly.

"But why send all this when they know we're behind?"

"Ballast and rails," Tim said evenly, "are ordered out on a schedule. By now, they will be sending no more but this was already on its way and could not be stopped."

He wheeled the buggy about and followed a rough construction road. They plunged into the forest and the track made a long curve to circle a hill. Phil critically studied the roadbed, the new and gleaming rails spiked to the ties. He wondered angrily why anyone should want to stop it.

Tim drove silently and grimly. They soon came on the true end-of-track. The rails abruptly ceased and beyond it stretched the roadbed, partially covered with the crushed rock ballast. Tim reined in.

"Watch 'em," he said tightly. "Ye'll see what's wrong."

At first Phil was puzzled. Track men placed the rails on the ties, the gauger made the adjustment and then the sledges drove home the heavy spikes that held them in place. Phil watched the men work to shape the roadbed itself, spread the ballast. It was a busy scene filled with movement and sound. Men cursed at the horses, called orders to the gangs working under them. Shovel men worked with a steady rhythm and dust billowed upward from the loose dirt.

Then he suddenly saw what Tim meant. These

men were working, true enough, but they worked as though each had a heavy ball and chain attached to his leg. Looking here and there, he saw men straighten, look around insolently and then slowly resume work. There was no push and drive, no hurry.

He saw the stacks of ties. They extended in on either side of the roadbed until they were lost around another curve. His attention centered on a work gang nearby. A foreman tried to hurry them along. One man looked grudgingly at the harried strawboss and deliberately spat to one side in an overt challenge. The foreman ignored it. Phil looked at Tim's tight face.

"I see what you mean."

"It ain't natural," Tim breathed. "Someone's told 'em this is the way to work."

"Who?" Phil demanded. "It doesn't make sense."

"Does that?" Tim made a gesture toward the workers.

Phil had no answer then, nor later when he returned to the hospital. The next day, despite Tim's and the doctor's protests, he had himself driven to Ensign. Tim drove slowly, so it was late in the evening before they arrived. Phil went directly to bed. He felt better the next morning. Tim came by early and they had breakfast. Later, Tim drove him to Fleming's office and the engineer was surprised to see Phil.

"Man, you should be in bed!"

"Can't afford that luxury," Phil said grimly. "I think I might have an answer to the problem. I'm going out to the ranch now, but I'll be back in a few days. Do I have that long?"

Fleming was honest. "You're so far behind now, Phil, that a day or two won't matter,"

"I'll take it then. Oh, you told Carol?"

"I told her," Fleming said flatly and Phil understood. His eyes grew bleak.

"Thanks."

By the time he arrived at the Flying W, he could do little more than sit in the big main room and listen to Farrell's report. The segundo was angry that someone had beaten Phil.

"We'll handle it pronto," Phil protested. "That's why I came here, especially. Get the work ahead of schedule. I'll be ready to ride in a couple of days."

Phil rested all he could, alternating rest with exercises designed to work the stiffness out of his muscles. The third day Farrell reported the Flying W could operate on a skeleton crew for a week and not be seriously handicapped.

"Good!" Phil exclaimed. "Tell the boys to check their Colts and their rifles and be ready to ride in the morning."

"You aim to pay off for that beating, Phil?"

"I aim to straighten up a construction camp."

Farrell grinned and eagerly left the ranch

house. The next morning Farrell and the crew waited. Each man wore holstered Colt and a rifle snugged at each saddle. They were a competent crew, Phil knew, and they could easily do the job he had in mind. He swung into the saddle. Without a word, he moved beside Farrell and started off on the trail toward town. They rode silently for a time, the only sound the creak of saddle leather and the dull thud of hoofs. Finally Farrell glanced at Phil.

"Where we headed and what are we going to do?"

"First to town," Phil replied, "and then we're going to hunt rats and wolves."

"Strange combination," Farrell laughed. "But I reckon it'll be fun."

XII

They rode fast, coming to Ensign just before noon, and Phil led the way directly to Tim's office. The big Irishman looked up in amazement at the armed riders.

"And what would this be?" he demanded.

"The answer to our problems," Phil said shortly. "Be ready to ride with us, Tim. I want to find Agren, and then we'll head directly out to the camp."

He stretched his aching muscles, decided the short walk to the mill would do him good. He strode down the main business block, passed saloons and a few stores, came on a millinery shop. As he neared the door, it opened and Carol Fleming stepped out onto the planked sidewalk. She stopped short when she saw Phil. He smiled and removed his hat.

"It's good to see you, Carol."

She smiled, but there was no real warmth in it. "I hope you have recovered, Phil."

"A few aches here and there."

"I'm glad to hear it. Now if you'll excuse me—"

She started around him. He impulsively put out his hand. She drew back but stopped nevertheless, cold and distant. His frown deepened.

"Carol, you treat me like a stranger, or more like—"

"A street brawler, Phil?" she asked.

"Carol!"

"I really must be getting on. I hope you fully recover." She gathered her skirt to make sure it didn't touch him, and walked away. His face flamed red, and anger swept through him. Now he knew the meaning of Fleming's flat voice when he said he had told his sister. He turned on his heel and strode on toward the sawmill, so angered and hurt that he trembled. Then reason came to his rescue. This was not like Carol. Despite what Fleming had told her, there must be someone else who had convinced her of the worse interpretation.

He was still in an angry mood when he climbed the slope to the sawmill and entered the office. Hal Agren labored at his desk. His coat hung on the chair behind him and his shirt looked startling white against the black vest he wore. He looked up when Phil entered.

"Phil Ward!" His voice sounded pleased and hearty as he extended his hand. "I heard they tried to kill you. Here, man, sit down." He pushed a chair beside his desk and forced Phil into it. "Tell me about it, Phil. I wanted to get up there but this place won't let me free for a minute."

Phil told him. Agren listened, apparently concerned. Now and then he'd make an angry comment. Phil might have warmed to this friendly interest, but there was something that did not quite ring true. He couldn't place it and yet it was there, as though Agren wore a mask that concealed his real feelings. He finished, feeling that he had told something Agren already knew.

"It certainly crippled your operations, Phil, being in the hospital. I hear you're falling far behind schedule."

"That's why I came here, Hal."

Agren involuntarily straightened, caught himself and spread his hands wide. "I don't understand, Phil. What do you want of me?"

"I've brought my punchers in from the ranch. I want to use all the men at the mill or from your lumber camps that you can spare."

"Why?"

"I'm cleaning out end-of-track, Hal. I need your help."

Agren leaned back and his fingers drummed lightly on the desk top. He shifted uneasily in his chair, tugged at his earlobe, dropped his hand and sighed. "Phil, I can't do it."

"Why not!"

"I can't spare a man. I've been given a lot of extra work in town. They're building stores and houses and they want the lumber. I'm filling those orders as fast as I can, so I'm only able to keep even with the railroad tie schedule."

"But I'm behind so far I'll not be able to use

your ties for a week. You can spare that much time."

Agren stubbornly shook his head. "Phil, whether you use those ties or not has no bearing on my contract with the railroad. I have to meet the schedule or I'm in breach of contract. You know that."

Phil leaned back, seething with anger again. He knew Agren was logically right, and yet Phil knew that the man simply did not want to help him. At the most he would lose a day and Hal could easily make it up by delaying some of the less pressing town orders. Phil felt himself blocked at every turn and knew he only wasted his time here. He pulled himself from the chair.

"All right, Hal. I'll do it myself and to hell with you."

Agren placed his hand on Phil's shoulder in a friendly gesture. "Phil, damn it! There's not a thing I can do about it, believe me."

Phil surrendered to the situation. Agren might be right at that, though Phil could not wholly bring himself to believe it. He smiled in acknowledgment, and Agren walked outside with him. He looked down the slope toward the town. "You'll be going to the camp right away?"

"I'll be there by nightfall."

"Then I wish you luck. Too bad you can't have supper with me at the Flemings' tonight. But I'm sure there'll be another time."

148

Phil gave him a sharp glance but Agren's face was clear. The allusion to the Flemings angered Phil again. He nodded curtly and walked away without a backward glance. He felt Agren's eyes follow him.

Farrell and the crew impatiently waited for him before Tim's office. Across the street a few curious loafers had gathered to watch but none dared question the grim, armed riders. Tim paced nervously back and forth and came hurrying to meet Phil.

"And what have ye learned?" he demanded.

"We'll get no help from Agren."

"*Whsst!* Did ye expect it? 'Tis only himself a man can depend on in time of trouble. Besides, Hal Agren has no liking for it when the road is rough."

"You're probably right, Tim. It's time we were riding."

They left Ensign, and Phil set a fast pace that would eat up the miles and yet not tire the horses. Night found them still some distance from the construction camp, but they rode on, grim shadows in the darkness. Near midnight, they broke out of the forest and saw the lights of the camp ahead, the greatest glow coming from the saloons and bordellos. Phil drew rein and the others crowded in close.

"We're riding through the camp to the far end," he said. "Farrell, you and Tim stay close to me.

The rest of you keep your eyes open, notice everything. I'll have more orders later."

They nodded and Phil straightened. "I don't think we'll have any trouble going through the camp, but be ready for it. Keep close up and pay no attention to anyone."

He wheeled his horse around, and led the way, Tim riding on one side, Farrell on the other, the big Flying W crew pressing close behind. They entered the first street, lined with bunkhouses. Lights glowed here and there. The few men looked at the grim cavalcade in astonishment as it rode by. Dark warehouses stood on either side, and ahead was the steady glow of light from end-of-track. Phil could hear the restless sound of the area even now, above the echoing fall of hoofs.

They came out into the glare and noise of end-of-track. As usual, it was crowded. Barkers called before the saloons and the walks were alive with workers moving from one place to another. They filled the street.

Phil did not slow and the silent men rode close behind him. The crowd broke before the cavalcade like water before the prow of a ship, and closed up behind it. Men stopped to stare on either walk and others skipped hurriedly out of the way of the riders, cursing them.

Phil rode stony faced, looking neither to the right nor to left. They passed the entrance to the alley of the cribs, then Pennard's High Iron. Phil's jaw set but he did not give the place a second glance. At last they reached the far edge of the camp and disappeared into the shadows beyond. Phil drew rein and again the men pressed close about him. His voice grew tight.

"All right. You've seen the place, all of it. We're going to ride through again. When we come out at the other side, I don't want to see a single saloon, gambling house, dancehall, or crib standing. We're pulling it down around their ears."

"Glory be!" Tim whispered, and the men stirred, tight smiles flashing across their grim faces. Phil continued.

"I want no gambler, barkeep, barker, dealer or whore in town by morning. I don't give a damn where or how they go—just drive them out. When dawn comes I want only the regular construction camp buildings standing."

"Sure, 'tis powerful medicine," Tim said. "There are some who have done no harm."

"They're all the same," Phil snapped.

He wheeled about to the camp, heading directly for the first tent saloon. The cavalcade halted before the door and all the men dismounted. Farrell quickly designated horse holders and the rest followed Phil into the saloon.

Their entrance instantly quieted the bedlam. Men turned from the bar, looked up from the poker tables. A dancehall girl took a single look at the grim strangers and swiftly muffled a scream. Phil felt the battery of questioning eyes on him.

"Take care of the bar," he said over his shoulder. "The rest of you follow me to the tables."

A bartender shouted an alarmed protest and another reached for a weapon below the bar. Farrell's gun blasted, and broken bottles showered the man. He ducked and forgot the concealed gun. Phil tipped over a green cloth table just as a thundering crash behind him signaled the destruction of the bar. Men yelled. Some acted as though they would fight but the grim, armed cowboys swiftly changed their minds. There was a sudden retreat and canvas ripped as a knife slit a quick exit. Wood splintered and glass crashed.

The owner popped out of his office, gun in his hand and his bouncers rallied beside him. But a group of Flying W men bore down on them, Colts leveled. A derringer exploded with a spiteful snap, to be answered by the roaring blast of a forty-four. A gambler grabbed his stomach and folded over. Boots pounded for the exits and there was no more resistance.

The Flying W men swept through the place, leaving total destruction behind them. As they left, the crowd that had gathered in the street dispersed, fleeing from the cowboys who went on to the next tent. Within a matter of minutes it collapsed and now a flickering of flames showed. Phil grabbed Tim.

"Get the bucket brigades ready to protect the main camp," he shouted above the pandemonium.

"Ye'd have me leave this fine brawl!" Tim protested.

"We've got to save the main buildings! Let this scum go up in smoke."

"I'll try," Tim said reluctantly. "Though there may not be a man-jack left back in the camp. Ye've ripped the place apart and they'll all be watching."

"Then force 'em to man the buckets," Phil snapped.

Tim faded away and Phil gave his attention to the business at hand. Now and then groups of the riffraff would form small knots of resistance. Sometimes they were aided by belligerently drunk construction workers. When this happened Phil or Farrell would gather a few of the cowboys and they'd break up the groups. There were amazingly few gunshots, though now and then some saloon bully boy or gun-slammer would resort to the Colt.

Flames licked hungrily behind the destroying cowboys. The panic spread as Phil led his men from tent to tent, from building to building. A row of crib houses caught fire as a fleeing woman knocked over a kerosene lamp. The dry wood caught like paper and soon the whole alley was ablaze. Phil watched the sparks lift and move across the night sky. The wind blew away from the main camp toward Devil's Canyon. It would not be hard to keep the blaze from the main buildings.

The fire became a more powerful force than the destroying punchers. The riffraff, frightened and confused, fled the area. A steady exodus of frightened, beaten gamblers, gunhawks, bartenders and women streamed out of the camp and fled along the road to Ensign, or across the trestle to the haven of the east side of Devil's Canyon.

The night sky was lurid with the lift of flames and streaming sparks. Joe Pennard's High Iron was broken up and splintered and soon the flames caught it. Phil searched the place for him or Braxton, but had no glimpse of either. They fled as fast as any of the spineless riffraff. It would be a long time, Phil thought with satisfaction, before Pennard would recover from this loss.

In the excitement, Phil forgot his bruises, though now and then he was vaguely aware that his side ached. The air was filled with smoke and sometimes embers would drop about Phil. But he went on. He had to use his gun twice. Several wild shots from the crowd came close, but there was no real opposition. He had struck so unexpectedly and so hard that there was no chance of the renegades' catching their balance. Panic added to panic and they were all caught up in it.

Then, abruptly, it was over. A small gambling

hall went up in flames and Phil looked ahead to see only the silent warehouses, the lights from the bunkhouses. He wearily passed his hand over his grimy face. The end of the street was packed with workers watching the destruction, silent and awed. Phil took a deep breath and called Farrell. The segundo joined him, his face a black mask through which his smile flashed white and startling.

"There ain't no more, Phil."

Phil nodded. "Bring up the horses. We're going to make sure the job is done."

XIII

Farrell called some of his riders to follow him. Phil realized that in the east there was a faint break of light, obscured by dirty, drifting clouds of smoke. Except for the crackle of the nearby flames there was a strange silence in the camp. A breeze picked up ashes, billowed them upward and then dispersed them in a shower of black and gray ash. Tim came, grinning widely.

"It's full job ye've done, bucko."

"Any fires in camp?"

"None." Tim blew on his knuckles. "It took me fist a few times to keep the lads at it. Ye've put the devil in his place, that I'll say."

Phil smiled wearily. "But the devil never stays there. I want all the work gangs assembled before they go out on the job."

Tim glanced at the sky, gray now with the coming morning. "It has been a long night, bucko boy. Ye'd best find yourself a bunk."

"Not yet. There's something else to be done."

Farrell came up and Phil gave orders to form a huge guard line about the camp. They were to make sure that none of the renegades of end-of-track would return. Satisfied, Phil walked with Tim to the foreman's cook shack.

There was a subdued air of excitement throughout the camp, but gradually routine resumed. Phil ate hungrily and drank several mugs of strong coffee. The others eyed him speculatively and talked among themselves in low tones. The superintendent came.

"Any change in plans?" he asked. Phil shook his head.

"Regular work day—after I've talked to the men."

The superintendent blurted, "That was a hell of a good job you did. Every railroad builder in the country will be thankful for it. No end-of-track town anywhere will ever get out of line again. You've shown what can be done."

He left, and Phil wearily glanced at the big clock on the far wall and pulled himself to his feet. Tim followed him outside. The camp was silent and deserted, every man having left for the meeting. Farrell drifted up, face drawn by weariness, but still triumphant.

"They're all waiting by the tracks."

"Gather the crew," Phil said, his jaw setting. "Spread 'em out around the crowd."

"Riding herd?" Farrell asked, surprised.

"Something like that, until the meeting breaks up."

Farrell rode away. Phil led the way to the construction office and found the superintendent waiting. Phil again glanced at the clock and hitched at his gunbelt.

"It's time we finished the job."

The open space between the camp and the gleaming new rails was filled with workers. They stood or milled about, curious, not sure after the night of destruction what would happen. The cordon of mounted, armed punchers about them increased their worry. A murmur swept through the crowd as Phil, Tim and the superintendent came up. Phil climbed onto an empty flatcar and looked over the crowd. Here and there a man nursed a hangover, or a face was marred by a bruise. Some looked sullen and angry, others frightened and nervous. Phil let the tension build up and then he spoke to them, evenly and forcefully.

"You've seen what happened to end-of-track. That's the end of it so far as I'm concerned." A low growl swept through the crowd and Phil raised his hands for silence. "There will be one or two saloons, but I'll decide who will run 'em and how long they stay open. But I didn't call you out to tell you this." He paused, letting them wonder what would come next. He saw several of them glance toward the Flying W men who ringed the group, sitting their horses, silent and threatening.

"I'm through playing," Phil said suddenly. "You get good wages, quarters and food. But someone in end-of-track had you slow down, made you discontented. Well, that's over. There'll be no

158

more free rotgut and twisted talk. There'll be no more drunken riots. If you have a hangover, you'd better not let it interfere with your work. You'll be fired."

He let that sink in. "I pay as good or better than any other contractor and every man-jack of you knows it. All right, you know where I stand and what's expected of you. If anyone doesn't like the terms, he can draw his pay right now. The rest of you can get back to your work."

He jumped down from the car. The men moved toward the camp and the tracks. They broke up into work gangs and within a few moments the meeting place was empty except for the Flying W men.

Phil was fairly staggering with weariness. Tim insisted that he rest and he did not have the energy to resist. He fell on a cot in the back room of the construction office and had hardly touched the rough blanket and pillow before his eyes were closed.

It was dark when he awoke. Someone had lit a lamp and he could hear the stir of men in the office beyond the thin partition. He sat up, rested, but groggy from the deep, exhausted sleep. He pulled himself to his feet and went into the main office.

Tim Moriarty sat at one of the desks, a contented expression on his moon face. The superintendent leafed through a pile of reports and two clerks worked at high ledger desks. All of them looked up when Phil appeared. Tim lowered the front legs of his chair to the floor with a bang.

"Sure, and ye look human, bucko."

Phil smiled. "Is everything quiet in the camp?"

The superintendent beamed and smacked his hand on the papers. "I'm going over the work reports. They read halfway decent."

"I have been through the camp," Tim said in a cheerful voice, "and 'tis a subdued bunch of spalpeens we have this night."

"The work?" Phil asked.

"Now some have quit," Tim said, still beaming, "and some have simply drifted off without so much as by your leave. But we have built roadbed and laid track this day as it should be done."

"Almost to schedule," the superintendent cut in.

Phil was pleased and said so. "But we've got to shoot ahead of schedule to make up for lost time."

"That we will," Tim answered forcefully. "I can now give my time to the hiring of decent men." He chuckled. "I'll give ye odds that half the country is filled with gamblers, bartenders and dance girls on the drift for new jobs. Sure, and they won't be coming back here after last night's work."

Tim went with Phil to have coffee, while Phil wolfed down a full meal. Farrell reported that the Flying W crew was resting but was ready to ride at a moment's notice. After eating, Phil wandered about the camp. There was a strange air of peace. Now and then a shift of the wind would bring the heavy odor of ashes from what had been end-of-track.

The next morning the camp emptied immediately after breakfast and, from the sound of it, Phil knew that the work picked up to its old rhythm. He gathered the Flying W men and they rode back to Ensign, where Phil told Farrell to let the men have a night on the town. He watched the men ride eagerly down the street to the saloons and then he went home.

He cleaned up. He felt a sense of accomplishment and the load of worry had lifted from his shoulders. He wondered where Joe Pennard and Braxton would be tonight and how they felt with their business wiped out and on the loose in a strange country. He hoped grimly that both of them had been taught a lesson.

He had dinner and walked along the main street, crowded at this hour of the evening. He turned in the direction of the Fleming house. He didn't like the idea of meeting Carol but he could make a report, assure the engineer that he need no longer worry about the building schedule, and leave as soon as that was done. Even so, he approached the house with reluctance.

He stepped up on the porch. He heard Fleming's deep voice through the screened door and then Carol's laugh. Phil braced himself and knocked.

There was an instant silence. The light streamed in the hall and he saw Carol coming toward him. She saw Phil and her stride broke momentarily. Then she hurried forward and opened the door.

"Phil! I'm so glad you came. We've been hearing about you."

"I'm sorry to break in," he said stiffly, "but I thought Rayburn—"

"Of course!" She flushed. "Phil, I was horrid the last time we met. Ray finally made me listen to him and now I know the situation you faced."

His heart lifted and for the first time in weeks he wanted to laugh aloud in sheer relief. "Things can get twisted, Carol. I don't blame you."

"But I blame myself." She smiled and took his arm, led him down the hall to the dining room. Fleming and Hal Agren sat at the table cleared of all but their coffee cups.

"Phil!" Fleming exclaimed and jumped up.

Agren arose more slowly. His eyes narrowed as he noticed Carol's hand resting lightly on Phil's arm. She hurried into the kitchen to bring coffee for Phil. Fleming forced him into a chair, throwing eager questions almost too fast to be answered.

They listened intently as Phil told them what had happened. Agren's fingers beat a soundless rhythm on the white table cloth. Fleming's eyes glowed and he nodded when Phil finished.

"We heard most of it, and strangely enough there wasn't too much story twisting this time."

He glanced sharply at Agren. "The town is filled with the riffraff you chased out."

"I'm sorry to inflict them on Ensign," Phil said.

"Most of them will drift on." Fleming frowned as a sudden thought hit him. "None of them have any love for you, Phil. I'd be mighty careful if I were you. Any of them would be damned glad to even the score."

"I never thought of that!" Carol exclaimed. "Do be careful, Phil!"

Agren's eyes lighted and he made a slight grimace as Carol impulsively touched Phil's arm again. Then the expressionless mask settled over his face.

"I won't worry too much about them. There's not a backbone in the whole lot."

"A coward with a gun is dangerous," Fleming warned.

Phil tried to dismiss it. He started to leave but both Fleming and Carol insisted that he stay. As the evening passed, Agren's face became more and more wooden. Phil obviously enjoyed himself and paid entirely too much attention to Carol. It was a return to the days when she had first come here, and Agren wondered if he was as secure in the girl's affections as he had thought. More than that, Phil had handled the crippling situation in an entirely unexpected way, and the plan had fallen through. Agren was forced to spend a couple of hours approving of Phil's actions when it meant that he had personally thrown a good deal of money to the winds. Cheap as Pennard's liquor had been, it still cost plenty when given freely to influence Phil's workers. It was a relief when Phil left.

Alone at last with Carol, Agren still found no real peace. He partially listened to her, his mind busy with Phil Ward. He finally pleaded weariness and a full day ahead and took his leave. . . .

It was still comparatively early, and Agren hurried to the main part of town. He paused on a corner and watched the crowd moving by. He glimpsed a harried gambler, moving aimlessly along, his hands shoved deep in his pockets. There were others like him and Agren wondered if they would like to get Phil Ward in the sights of a gun. The thought encouraged him and he turned sharply, walking to the Navajo Bar with renewed purpose.

It was filled with refugees from the end-of-track camp. All of them were angry, morose and discouraged. Agren moved through the crowd and, at a back table, saw his man. Joe Pennard's sallow horse face looked weary and lined. His clothes were rumpled and his eyes held a wicked, angry look. Agren gave a quick, cautious look around the crowded room and slipped into one of the vacant chairs.

"A hell of a deal you and Reiger cooked up!" Pennard growled.

"It went wrong," Agren hastily said.

"You're damn right it went wrong! I'm wiped out."

Agren caught a waiter's eyes and ordered a bottle. Pennard growled under his breath and then eagerly filled his glass when the bottle was thudded down on the table. Agren waited until the man had two quick drinks.

"It's not as bad as you think, Joe," he said. "We'll see that you're not too badly hurt."

"Fine promises," Pennard sneered. Agren made an impatient gesture.

"But there's something you can do tonight. I'll pay high for it."

"What?" Pennard demanded. "Get Phil Ward riding my back again?"

"No, getting rid of him." He glanced around again and then pulled out a roll of bills. He peeled off several yellow backs and put them before Pennard, speaking quickly and incisively. Pennard listened, skeptically at first and then with increasing interest. He rubbed his hand along his jaw, his thick lips twisting thoughtfully. Finally he nodded and picked up the bills.

"Won't hurt to try, and I know Braxton. The dinero will help, anyhow, win or lose."

Agren started to protest, thought better of it. He moved through the crowd and out into the street. He smiled as he looked back at the saloon and then started for home.

Phil Ward found most of his punchers lining the bar of the Last Dollar Saloon. Farrell sat at a table with three punchers, playing stud poker. The men were relaxed and cheerful and Phil spoke to several of them as he worked through the crowd to the table. Farrell looked up, grinning.

"Any more camps to burn?" he asked.

"None right now. I thought you'd had enough of it."

"Always look forward to a little excitement," one of the men said. "Rounding up dogies will be mighty damn monotonous now."

"But that's what you'll do," Phil grinned. "Take 'em back to the ranch come morning, Farrell. Maybe range riding will work the humps out of their backs."

"I'll try it, anyhow," Farrell nodded.

Phil watched the game for a while, and had a drink at the bar with the men. He left the saloon and walked slowly to his house.

It seemed that he had just closed his eyes when he was awakened by a knocking on the door, not loud but steady. Phil's eyes opened and he swung out of bed. He fumbled in the darkness for his gunbelt and pulled the Colt from the holster. He walked silently to the door.

"Who is it?" he called.

"Mr. Fleming sent me."

The voice sounded young. Phil unlocked the

door and leveled the Colt as he opened it. A boy of about fifteen faced him. His eyes widened when he saw the gun muzzle lined on his stomach. He swallowed with difficulty and Phil instantly lowered the weapon.

"Fleming sent you?"

The boy recovered his voice. "Yes, sir. He said something had gone wrong and for you to meet him at his office right away."

The boy hurried off. Phil hastily dressed, wondering what had happened at the camp. It would be bad or Fleming would not arouse him. Maybe some of the renegades had struck back. He buckled on his gunbelt, jammed on his hat and left the house.

On the main street a single light glowed in a saloon. The air had a cold bite that would leave only when the sun came up. The railroad office was dark and Phil looked about for Fleming, but no one was in sight. He peered in either direction along the street, half expecting to see the engineer. The man would have undoubtedly brought horses. But nothing stirred.

Phil suddenly straightened, alert. He wished he had questioned the lad more closely. Phil stepped to the edge of the planked walk, still half expecting Fleming.

An orange flame leaped toward him from the shadows across the street. Phil heard the spiteful whine of the bullet, and felt a tug at the sleeve high up on his left arm.

XIV

Phil dropped into a crouch and sprang for the shadow of the office building. The gun thundered again, the bullet seeking him out. He heard it smack into the wall a few inches away.

He slammed a shot in reply. Once more the orange flame spat toward him and gun thunder echoed. Phil crouched low in the shadows, eyes narrowed in an effort to find the ambusher.

He waited, Colt poised, hammer dogged back. He saw the faint move of a shadow in the narrow space between two buildings. Phil took a split second to make sure of his aim. He squeezed the trigger and the weapon bucked against his hand. He sent a second shot and a third, deliberately placing them to cover the area where he was sure the killer lurked.

There was a sudden spasmodic movement over there, but no answering reply. Phil darted away from the office, running crouched. He expected a shot but he reached the opposite walk in safety. He was now out of the man's line of fire and the ambusher would have to step out on the walk to target him.

Phil threw two more slugs at the dark shadows, wheeled and raced down a narrow passageway to the alley. He hastily ejected spent shells and reloaded. The ambusher now lurked on the far side of the building beside which Phil crouched. Phil now had a chance to come up on him from the rear.

He cautiously moved around the corner and along the back of the building. He still had several feet to go when a man suddenly erupted from around the other corner, looking back over his shoulder, unaware of Phil. There was a subdued glint of metal in his hand, a Colt.

Phil leveled his gun and pulled the trigger. The man was flung back in a tangle of arms and legs. He clung against the corner of the building for a moment and his gun blasted, the flame lancing toward the ground. It was purely reflex action, for the man suddenly fell forward, sprawling on his face.

Phil waited, gun still leveled, thumb dogging the hammer. He feared a trap or a trick. Then he heard a rasping, labored breathing and he knew the man was hard hit. Phil moved forward, alert and tense, and stood over the dark figure, gun ready.

The man did not move. His breathing made a gurgling whisper in the sudden stillness of the night. Phil heard an alarmed shout from the street beyond the building. He rolled the man over, fumbled for a match and struck it. The flame revealed Braxton's tortured features. A dark stain spread over his shirt front and his eyes stared up at Phil. The match flame snapped out but Phil did not strike another.

"Pennard sent you," he said flatly. "You're done for and you might as well tell the truth. Pennard sent you."

There was another long silence and then Braxton whispered hoarsely, "Joe . . . sent me. Get even for—"

"Losing his saloon," Phil said when Braxton did not finish. "A hell of a thing to die for, Braxton."

"A hell . . . of a thing to die—" Braxton's whisper was weaker. "But not that alone. Joe—someone else—rancher."

"Who?" Phil demanded sharply. Braxton's voice faded.

"Rancher—sawmill."

His breathing expelled in a long sigh. Phil hastily struck another match and the brief flame showed that Braxton was dead. Boots pounded and men erupted around the corner of the building. Phil turned as they came charging up. He caught the glint of a star on the shirt of the first man.

The sheriff asked swift, pointed questions and Phil answered. Someone in the crowd recognized Braxton and confirmed Phil's statement that he was one of the gunhawks driven out of the construction camp. The lawman recovered Braxton's gun and ejected the spent shells into his hand. He looked at Phil grimly.

"You were lucky none of these had your name."

"Very lucky." Phil showed the jagged tear in his sleeve. He indicated the gun. "May I have it, Sheriff? I know someone who'd like to see it."

The lawman shrugged and gave him the weapon. He dispersed the crowd, sending one of the men to arouse the undertaker. He released Phil.

"You saved the Territory the cost of a trial and a hanging. Men like Braxton always end up this way—or dead in an alley. But be careful, Ward. This is just a sample. You've made a lot of enemies."

Phil nodded soberly, thanked the sheriff, and walked back to the street. He was still keyed up and knew that it would be futile to go to bed. He thought of what Braxton had said and he didn't like the implications . . . he could hardly believe it. Joe Pennard was behind Braxton, but the gunhawk had revealed that there were yet others behind Pennard. This could explain why the saloonkeeper gave away his poisonous liquor. And mental poison against Phil went with each glass handed across the bar.

A rancher behind Pennard—Braxton had been clear on that score. Only Milt Reiger hated Phil enough to work out some involved scheme like this. Reiger wanted the contract and, losing it, he still tried to gain his ends by other means. Phil was only surprised that Dave Trego hadn't gunned for him.

Phil looked down the dark street, hardly noticing the few lights. There was a sudden flurry of voices as the undertaker and his assistant came out, bearing a long wicker basket. Phil's lips flattened and he lifted Braxton's gun, studying its dull blue shine.

Phil began to have more respect for Reiger, who had obviously tried to ruin him by slowing the work on the railroad. Yet at no time had Reiger exposed his hand. Phil could accuse only Pennard. Now Braxton had tried murder, and Braxton had lost. The trail led to Pennard and stopped.

Phil's thoughts turned to the other word Braxton had used: "sawmill." That could only mean Hal Agren. The man was jealous of Carol, and maybe rightly so. He was ambitious and driving, but Phil could hardly believe that he would be involved with renegades and gunhawks. Phil frowned darkly. This explained Agren's strange attitudes and remarks, that subtle antagonism that Phil had often sensed.

Phil hefted Braxton's gun. He'd get to the bottom of this, but right now there was something else he must do. He looked down the street. Pennard undoubtedly had heard the gunshots, and would know that his killer had struck. Phil thrust Braxton's Colt behind his belt buckle.

He walked down the street to the one lighted saloon. He paused just outside the door and shifted his holster to an easier position, then he pushed open the batwings.

A single customer was at the bar. Phil's hard eyes swept over the rows of empty tables. Pennard sat silent and tense against the far wall, staring at Phil as though he couldn't quite believe his eyes. Phil slowly threaded among the tables, and come to a halt before Pennard. The man's sallow skin was shiny and sweaty in the lamplight, his face drawn and lengthened. He kept his hands in plain sight on the table and his murky eyes watched Phil with ill-concealed fear.

"You stay up late, Joe," Phil said evenly. Pennard's eyes darted to the door, back to Phil.

"There's nothing else to do. You saw to that."

"You sang a different tune the last time we met, Joe. Who paid for the rotgut you gave away?"

Pennard's eyes flicked, no more. He gained a last ounce of confidence. "You don't make sense."

"Was it Milt Reiger?" Phil insisted. "Or someone else?"

"You talk crazy," Pennard said shortly. His eyes darted to the batwings again.

"You're lying, Joe. You wanted the work to stop, and that never made sense from the beginning. The more pay the men drew, the more money you could milk from them."

"Maybe I wanted to get out of the saloon business," Pennard said, "so I gave the stuff away."

173

"So when I bring the place down around your ears and drive you out," Phil said flatly, "you try to even the score."

"You're still talking crazy."

Phil reached inside his coat and Pennard's fingers pressed the green table top. Phil pulled out the Colt and placed it carefully on the table. The man's eyes dropped to it, fascinated. Then he slowly looked up.

"Braxton's," Phil said quietly. "He tried, but he missed. You can see him at the undertaker's. But you've only got until tomorrow noon to see him."

Pennard licked his lips and a touch of defiance came to his eyes, then vanished. Phil's smile was harsh and grim. "Just until noon, Joe. If you're in Ensign after that, you'll be in a wooden box beside Braxton."

"You can't—"

"But I can, Joe. If you want to stay alive, be a hell of a long way out of Ensign." Phil pointed to the gun. "It's not loaded, Joe, in case you have some idea of shooting me in the back when I leave. In fact, I hope you try it."

He turned toward the door. His steps sounded loud in the silent room and he felt Pennard's hateful glance. The batwings whispered behind him and Phil felt tired, bone weary, and his side began to ache. He went home, undressed and stretched out on the bed.

But he couldn't sleep. He saw the gun flashes in

the night street; Joe Pennard's eyes filled with fear, hate and something of a challenge; heard Braxton's hoarse and gasping voice. Phil's mind centered on the fact that the gunhawk had implicated Hal Agren.

Phil rolled restlessly to one side and tried to dismiss it. Agren had his faults—too confident, too boastful, inclined to shade off the corners when he was sure no one watched. But Phil could still not quite bring himself to believe this about the man, despite Braxton's dying words. Phil's mind churned and moved in circles until he drifted off into a restless sleep.

He awoke feeling as tired as when he had gone to bed. The uncertainty and worry about Agren struck him again. He tried to judge it in the cold light of day and found that his suspicions had strengthened.

He had breakfast and then went first to Tim's office. Tim had heard about the shooting and was all for cleaning out Ensign. Phil dissuaded him, sure there would be no further attempts and saying that Pennard would be gone within a matter of hours. He brought the talk around to the day's problems and Tim soon forgot the matter in his enthusiasm to get the railroad back on schedule.

At last the business at the office was wound up and Phil left. He heard the whine of the saw-mill above the noise of the crowd. Phil's head lifted. Why carry suspicion of Agren around all day? His eyes grew bleak, but he walked to the mill.

The place was humming, and the office was filled. Agren handled customers at the counter and he had time only to motion Phil to the chair beside his desk. Phil waited, studying Agren, listening to his voice. He didn't act or sound like a man who'd plot another's ruin or death. Phil had an impulse to walk out, but something held him. At last the morning rush ended and Agren came to the desk, a sheaf of lumber orders in his hand.

"I never thought Ensign needed so damn much wood!"

"You're lucky." Phil glanced at the clerks. "I want to talk to you alone."

Agren had started to sit down, but he checked poised above the chair. Something flicked through his eyes and was gone. His smile remained wide and friendly.

"Can't it wait? We're mighty busy, and Carol's coming in a short time. I promised her a ride in the woods."

"It can't wait, Hal. It's personal."

Agren sat down, his handsome face petulant. He toyed with a pencil and spoke briefly to the clerks, who left the office. Agren swung his chair around and faced Phil.

"All right. What is all this mystery?"

"Do you know Joe Pennard or his gunslinger, Braxton?"

"Never heard of 'em," Agren answered readily. It came too quickly and there was a slight flicker in the eyes that Phil did not miss. Agren's fingers could not be still, dog-earing papers, picking up a pencil, dropping it.

"Last night, Braxton tried to drygulch me. I was lucky, Hal. I killed him before he killed me."

Agren sat frozen, his eyes searching Phil's face. There was something wrong in them. They were not as surprised or as innocent as Agren tried to make them. He swallowed.

"That's terrible, Phil! A man's not safe—"

"Braxton didn't die right away," Phil cut in. Agren's mouth hung open and there was a reddening along the back of his neck. Phil's voice became expressionless. "He talked."

Agren swallowed again. His eyes would not meet Phil's. He must have planned it! Phil thought, amazed even though he'd had forewarning.

"Braxton said Pennard operated at end-of-track on the orders of a rancher."

"Why, man, that means someone we know!" Agren exclaimed.

Phil's eyes remained cold and level. "Braxton also said there was someone connected with a sawmill behind Pennard. Did he mean you, Hal?"

The sudden blaze of fear and guilt in the man's eyes was answer enough. Phil stared at him in growing horror. He lurched to his feet and Agren shrank back. Phil's voice strangled but the words jerked out.

"You tried to ruin me! You backed this bush-whack last night!"

"That's a lie, Ward!"

He wheeled. Carol stood in the door, her face white and her eyes blazing. One hand still held the knob and the other was clenched into a small fist. She was dressed for riding, a linen duster over her dress, a pert hat atop the golden hair, the veil making a lovely pattern on her pale face. She took a step into the office.

"What are you trying to do!" she demanded.

Phil was painfully embarrassed that she should have overheard, but he tried to explain what had happened, what Braxton had said. Carol's anger mounted as she brushed the whole thing aside with blazing contempt.

"You'd take the word of a murderer! You'd believe a scum from end-of-track! You should've known better!"

She continued, angered beyond thought. Phil suddenly caught Agren's expression. He watched Carol, eyes alight, surprised and delighted at this unexpected ally. He made no move to defend himself but allowed the girl to do it. Phil had the perfect picture of a man retreating behind the protection of a woman's love. Phil knew he was guilty; there were too many signs.

Carol finally ended, breathless, beautiful in her anger. She stood between Phil and Agren, her body taut, arms rigid and fists clenched as she glared at Phil. Agren placed his hand on her shoulder and he looked in sly triumph at Phil.

"Darling, there's no need to even answer him. He hasn't a shred of proof. I can't understand him unless he's so jealous of you—"

"What!" Phil's voice snapped. He took a deep breath, knowing he dared not stay longer. He whipped about on his heel and strode to the door, flung it open. He turned back to the man and the woman, eyes locking with Agren's mocking gaze.

"Maybe I can't prove a thing. But I'll give you a warning. Watch your step."

"You can't talk—" Carol started and Phil's wrath swung to her.

"You're blind, Carol. If you marry this man—"

"I intend to," she said, her chin lifting. Phil's anger washed out of him. He looked at Agren, then pityingly at her. He shrugged and his voice became soft.

"That's too bad, Carol. I wish you luck." A muscle suddenly jumped in his lean jaw. "You're sure as hell going to need it."

He left, slamming the door behind him.

XV

Anger was a spur and a torture to Phil. He knew beyond doubt now that for some reason Hal Agren had turned against him. He had no proof, as Agren had so complacently assured Carol, but the conviction remained. He still could not determine all Agren's motives but one of them was his jealousy over Carol.

And Carol! Phil's cheeks flamed and he was angry that he should be embarrassed. Damn it, why should he feel shame at uttering the truth? He knew it was because he had hurt Carol. Agren should have asked her to leave but, instead, had used her so effectively that Phil had retreated before anger and scorn. Phil felt trapped in a false position.

He could not rid himself of inner turmoil no matter how fast he walked. He tried to calm himself with a drink at the closest bar. He glanced up at the clock to see that it pointed to noon. His eyes lighted and he hitched at his gunbelt.

Phil started a methodical round of the other saloons, looking for Joe Pennard. He asked sharp questions. No one had seen Pennard since early morning. Phil restlessly prowled the streets, but the ex-saloonkeeper had evidently left town. By mid-afternoon Phil had a grim sense of satisfaction. There was no trace of Pennard and he was satisfied that his warning had been heeded. It was at least one small thing breaking his way.

By the time he was ready to go to bed that night, Phil had achieved a certain amount of balance. He was no longer blazing angry at Carol. He wondered how she could be awakened to Hal Agren before she wrecked her life. There seemed to be no answer. She would not listen to Phil and she would spring to Agren's defense no matter from what source the accusation came. Only something that Agren himself might do would prove his true nature.

More important was Phil's own situation now that he knew Agren worked against him. He lay in the dark room and checked the ways by which Agren might strike at him again. Agren would not take the chance of another failure. How else could he strike? Phil couldn't forsee any method at the moment but he did not allow this to give him a false sense of security. Agren was clever. He fell asleep still trying to worry out the problem. . . .

The next morning after breakfast a Flying W rider hurried into the office looking for him. He swiftly gave Phil the news. "Farrell wants you at the ranch right away. We got trouble."

"What is it?"

"Rustling, looks like."

Phil's jaw set. He left instructions for Tim and then rejoined the puncher. In a few moments they rode fast out of town, taking the trail to the Flying W. Brant Farrell waited for him. Phil dismounted and led the way to the ranch office, where Farrell grimly gave the details.

"At least a hundred head," he reported. "They had been gathered before we left for town so we could distribute them to the lumber camps."

"Anyone riding herd?" Phil asked. Farrell shook his head.

"We had 'em in a box canyon, a fence across the mouth. We've done that before, Phil, but we never had rustlers."

"I know. I don't blame you. How about sign?"

"We trailed 'em as far as we could and the beef was run into the broken country, the trail as plain as Ensign's streets. Then they pulled an old Indian trick. They scattered and there were fifty trails to follow, and they got mighty careful about signs."

"When did it happen?"

"While we were at end-of-track."

"Someone was watching us," Phil said and Farrell nodded. Phil paced to the window, back to the desk. "How do we stand now on the delivery schedule?"

"The boys are rounding up enough to make it," Farrell said. "I'm not worried about that—this time. But a hundred head is a hell of a loss, Phil, and if this happens regular we're in trouble."

Phil nodded. "Let's get on the job."

They rode directly to the box canyon. There

was a stout wire fence built across its mouth, but Farrell picked up the broken strands, cut clean and sharp. Farrell then showed Phil where mounted men had driven off the beef.

Phil bleakly nodded. They followed the trail into the broken country toward the west. The cattle had been driven hard. Then sign suddenly broke up, scattering. At this point half a dozen Flying W riders had made a small camp to wait for Farrell and Phil. A lanky puncher, Red Neve, wearily thumbed his hat back from his face.

"We've each followed one of them trails," he said disgustedly. "Every one fades out. Them rustlers must've been trained by Apaches. There just ain't no way to follow 'em."

"We'll see," Phil said. He dismounted, stretched his tired muscles and accepted a hot mug of coffee. The other men confirmed Red's statement. The various trails vanished. Red made a sweeping motion west and northward.

"There's a hell of a lot of country up there, and all of it mean. It'd take an army to track down each separate trail."

Phil returned the mug with a gesture of finality. "So we'll try to follow one."

"Won't work," Red said flatly.

"You could be right. But it's all we can do. Let's ride."

They chose the most likely of the scattered trails, though with no real hope of being able to follow it for long. Phil nevertheless set them on it and they moved into the labyrinth of canyons and draws. As Red had warned, the trail disappeared within three miles and the men drew rein in a small knot about Phil.

He looked about the low crowned hills on every side. He pictured the country, trying to determine the most likely place that cattle could be driven. He was sure that somewhere these trails would again merge into one when the rustlers felt they were safe. The problem was to find that point of convergence.

"There's no point trying the impossible," Phil said slowly. "This sign wipes out, so we'll work the whole area, spreading out. Each man take a draw and work westward."

"Look for sign?" Red asked dubiously.

"For the place where they met again," Phil corrected. "If one of you finds it, fire two shots."

"Makes sense," Farrell agreed.

The group fanned out, each rider disappearing down a draw. Phil stayed with Farrell. The hours dragged by without a signal. The sun sank westward and Phil felt a deep sense of discouragement. Night would catch them scattered.

Farrell's bleak face reflected Phil's discouragement. As Red had said, the rustlers must have been Apache-trained. Suddenly Farrell and Phil jerked erect. Two shots sounded, and they were not far away. Farrell's face broke into a wide grin.

"Well, what do you know!"

Phil necked reined the horse, set the spurs, darting up a canyon in the direction of the shots. The ride was fast and twisting. The two shots came again, this time from just over the next ridge. The canyon made another sharp turn and Phil plunged into a little open meadow, the hub of a series of converging canyons. Three riders waited, dismounted.

"They met here," Red said triumphantly. "Sign's all around."

He made a wide gesture. Farrell and Phil swung out of their saddles. Red pointed northwest, toward a narrow defile.

"They drove the whole herd that way."

Phil frowned. "There's nothing up there but Grand Canyon rim."

"Maybe some hiding place," Farrell said grimly, "where they change the brands before they scatter 'em out to a dozen ranches."

That sounded reasonable. More riders came up and they held an eager consultation. Phil looked at the western peaks, golden with the sun that had now dropped below them. He spoke regretfully.

"In less than an hour it'll be too dark to follow trail. We might as well wait until morning."

They made camp, reluctantly, but at dawn they were up and had breakfast. As soon as it was light enough to see the trail again, they were in the saddle, pushing down the narrow canyon where the track lay plain and clear. It led straight for a few miles and then, surprisingly, veered eastward. Phil thought the rustlers might be doubling back to a rendezvous. Farrell hazarded the guess the hide-out might actually be on Flying W range.

"There're places we haven't seen in months," he admitted. "We don't run beef in the bad country and there's no reason for any of us to ride there unless we're chasing drifters."

Then the trail changed directions again, heading south. Farrell drew rein and looked ahead, frowning, puzzled.

"It doesn't make sense."

Phil had no answer, either, but grimly indicated that they should continue to follow. A few miles further, the trail turned west again, doubling on itself. Red spoke the puzzled thoughts of the others.

"They must be drunk, or crazy. They're sure wasting a lot of time."

Late in the afternoon they had the answer. They rode up a long draw that made a sharp angle around a ridge. Phil and Farrell led the group and they rounded the turn and came into a small meadow. Phil's face turned pale and with an oath, he drew rein.

Farrell's surprised curse sounded a moment later. The others stared, stunned and amazed. There on the meadow was the stolen herd, every head of it. Not a creature was on its feet. They lay scattered all over the meadow.

"My God!" Farrell exclaimed.

Phil rode slowly to the nearest animal. It had been shot through the head and left where it had fallen, otherwise untouched. Silently Farrell and the punchers rode from one carcass to another. It was the same story, wanton killing and destruction. Phil joined the silent group at the far side of the meadow.

Farrell spoke in a gusty whisper. "What kind of a man could do that!"

"No rustlers," Phil said through set teeth. "They didn't want to steal beef. They wanted to ruin the Flying W."

"Who?" Farrell demanded.

"I think I know. We'll find out. Let's find the trail again."

The men scattered into the mouths of the small canyons radiating outward. Almost immediately one of them yelled and swung his hat over his head. Phil set the spurs and raced around the beef carcass, Farrell and the others right behind him. The puncher pointed up the canyon.

"They went up here, maybe eight of 'em."

Again the sign was clear for the length of the canyon and then it became more difficult to follow. The men ahead had started to take pains to cover their trail. Still Red and Farrell managed to follow it until darkness brought a halt again.

This time there was no relaxation around the fire. Each man saw the wanton destruction back there in the meadow. They ate, talked briefly and then rolled up in their blankets. Breakfast at daybreak was just as silent and quick and soon they were in the saddle again.

The trail grew increasingly hard to follow and then the renegades resorted to the old Indian trick again. Each man rode off in a different direction, taking pains to leave no sign. Farrell hopelessly turned to Phil.

"There's no chance now. These owlhooters are riding alone. You might as well try to track a hawk through the sky."

Phil glared at the ground as though he could force it to give up its secret, futile anger a heavy pressure in his chest. They were far to the north and west of the home ranch now, beyond the actual boundaries of the Flying W. All the rustlers who had scattered had headed in a general direction, and Phil's eyes narrowed. He looked around at the men, again noting their holstered guns, their tight and angry looks.

"Forget the trail, Brant. We're paying a visit."

"Where?"

"Reiger!" Phil snapped.

They rode swiftly, headed in a straight line for Reiger's home ranch. Farrell looked questioningly at Phil several times but said nothing. Phil knew what he thought and agreed with him. This ride had nothing more than a hunch to back it.

Toward midday they came into a wide valley, and down a gentle slope they saw the cluster of buildings that marked Reiger's ranch. They drew rein and Phil studied the place. Now that he could actually see it Phil's anger boiled anew. He started down the slope, the men following him.

Phil set a steady pace. They were still some distance away when a group of riders suddenly appeared around the buildings and galloped toward them. Phil discovered Reiger's stocky figure, Dave Trego close beside him.

"They expected us," Farrell said.

"Maybe," Phil answered. "Be ready for trouble."

Reiger suddenly reined in and the hardcase riders about him pulled to a dust-raising halt. They waited, their stillness ominous. Phil made sure that his Colt would slip easily out of the holster. Farrell slid his rifle out of the scabbard, placed it across the saddle before him. Phil reined in several yards from the bunched Lazy R men.

His sharp eyes swept across them. Their horses looked as if they had not been ridden but these men would have had time to change mounts by now. No proof here that Reiger had anything to do with the dead cattle, but Braxton's words kept ringing in Phil's ears. Reiger's jaw was set, his square face harsh. Trego slouched easily, but his right hand remained close to his gun. The mocking eyes set deep in the skull-like face watched Phil closely.

"Ain't you strayed some?" Reiger asked.

"No," Phil snapped. His men waited, tense and ready, and the sun caught the glint of the rifle barrels resting across their saddles.

"A visit?" Reiger asked in mocking surprise. "Lose something?"

"Yes," Phil answered. He caught Trego's grin, the mocking triumph Reiger could not entirely keep out of his voice.

"Now ain't that a surprise!"

"Is it? We found around a hundred head of Flying W beef deliberately shot and left to rot."

"Now who'd do a thing like that!" Reiger exclaimed.

"I think you'd do it," Phil snapped.

"That'd be mighty damn hard to prove," Reiger replied, "since any of the boys here'll say none of us has left the ranch."

"Then you'd all be lying."

Reiger stiffened and instantly Flying W rifles shifted slightly. Reiger eased his weight back in the saddle.

"You talk damn big," he growled.

"I'm going to talk bigger. I can't prove a thing about the cattle, or about what happened at my construction camp." Reiger's eyes flickered. "But

Pennard's gunhawk, Braxton, did some talking before he died. I drove Pennard out of town."

"What's that got to do with me?" Reiger demanded.

"I'll not argue," Phil said sharply. "But I'm giving you a warning, Reiger. The next time I find a single head of my beef missing or dead, I'll string you up on the nearest tree."

Trego jerked upright, but he checked the downward plunge of his hand. Farrell's voice sounded cold and harsh.

"Go ahead, Dave. I'd like to blast you out of the saddle."

Phil watched Reiger, hoping for some reaction. But the rancher made no move, though his face was suffused a dull red and his eyes sparked hate. Finally Phil took a deep breath.

"Just remember what I've told you, Reiger. You've been pushing for trouble and now you'll get it. That's a promise."

He neck-reined his horse and rode away. In a moment Farrell and the other boys joined him. Phil didn't look back but he knew Reiger, Trego and the renegades had not moved.

Phil had a nagging suspicion that he had not done enough. Threats would not deter Reiger. He should have finished the job there and then.

XVI

Phil headed back to the home ranch, and the grim bunch of riders finally turned their mounts into the corral. Later that day Brant Farrell came to the office where Phil checked over the ranch records. Farrell slumped into a chair and Phil turned from the desk.

"You took a long chance with Reiger," Farrell said; "something like poking a bear with a stick. That kind always has a new trick."

Phil nodded. "We'll watch for it. Better keep a close watch, Brant."

"I've already taken care of the line riding."

"That's good, Brant. I don't think Reiger will take the chance, but we'll watch him just the same."

Phil remained at the Flying W for almost a week, but there was no further sign of trouble. Phil set up a quickened delivery schedule for the beef so that the loss of the hundred head would be covered. He was not wholly satisfied that all was peaceful on the range when he finally rode back to Ensign. But he had to watch that angle of his contract, too, and he knew that Farrell could handle anything that came up.

Ensign was peaceful, and a check with Tim assured Phil that things went smoothly, at least on the surface. The labor turnover had noticeably dropped and the work reports showed that the construction went ahead at top speed.

"Give us another couple of weeks," Tim said, "and the boys will be coming right into Ensign. We're already setting up a camp just west of town."

In order to keep the work going, this second camp would mean more business for Agren. As soon as the men moved into the new camp, the old one would be dismantled, moved further west, and set up again. At no time would the men have far to go to their work and there would not be even a day's delay in moving. He decided to check the camp.

The next day he rode out. The roadbed now extended several miles east of the camp and Phil watched the work for a long time. He could see the difference. The men moved with a new precision, and worked willingly and hard. The foreman no longer fought to keep up with the schedule. Phil conferred with several of them and was pleased.

The superintendent and the railroad engineers had the same glowing reports. They had caught up with the schedule and were now hopeful that before long they would exceed it.

"We're back to a mile a day," the superintendent told Phil. "If we keep that up, we'll reach the Colorado ahead of time."

Phil laughed at his optimism. "You're covering a lot of miles and a lot of problems."

"Sure, but we've got good workers, thanks to Tim Moriarty."

The superintendent suddenly checked. "Want to see the new end-of-track?"

"It's back?" Phil exclaimed, startled.

"Let's take a look."

End-of-track was nothing like the place that Phil had cleaned out. There were just three large tent saloons and he suspiciously entered them. They were clean and orderly. Two of the owners had been long established in Ensign.

Phil returned to the camp office feeling that by some strange miracle his troubles had all faded away. There would always be minor problems, he knew, but perhaps nothing like he had been forced to deal with in the past.

He remained overnight. The men flocked to the saloons; they drank and they gambled, but there was none of the frenzy Phil had seen before and he was surprised when at a fairly early hour all three saloons disgorged their customers and their lights went out. He spoke of this to the superintendent the next day.

"It's their contract with Moriarty," the man explained. "If they want to stay in business, they follow the rules."

Phil spent the day checking the warehouses, making sure of supplies. He finally leaned back and wearily passed his hands over his eyes. Building a railroad, he thought, sounded simple enough. Until you tried it.

He slept soundly that night despite the press of a thousand details. After an early breakfast he started back to Ensign, cheerfully hopeful. Only Carol worried him. He thought regretfully of her and wished that this part of his life might have worked out differently. But Carol was definitely in love with Hal Agren and would probably marry him. Phil wondered if he would ever again meet a girl who would mean as much to him. He cast these thoughts out of his mind. There was no use dwelling on that.

As Phil rode toward Ensign, three men sat in the bunkhouse of a lumber camp not far from the Lazy R. Hal Agren paced angrily and Reiger glowered at greasy cards on the wooden table before him. Dave Trego sat on one of the bunks against the wall. Agren wheeled about, scowling at Reiger.

"We've lost twice, Milt."

"Bad luck," Reiger growled.

Agren threw his arms wide in an angry, impatient gesture. "Bad luck! What a hell of a way to say it!" Agren jerked one of the rough chairs back and sat down at the table. "We could do this easy, remember? You could handle the whole deal if I'd furnish the money. Ward would be broke and you'd take over the ranch and the beef, I'd take over the railroad contract."

Reiger looked up from under his brows, his face flushing. "That was the idea."

"So Pennard bungles the job—"

"And you get a bright idea a bushwhack will take care of everything. Braxton bungled. You can't blame *that* on me."

Trego stirred. "No point in calling names," he said reasonably. "I can't see that it'll brand any strays."

"He's right," Reiger said.

Agren slowly eased back in his chair. "We've either got to forget the whole deal or do something damn quick."

"Easy said," Reiger glowered out the open door where tree shadows made changing patterns.

"It has to be done," Agren's fist struck the table. "I want him out of the game before he has the satisfaction of putting a single rail in town."

"Why so eager all of a sudden?" Trego asked dryly.

Agren started to answer, but changed his mind. He thought of Carol, so quick to defend him, but he believed that despite herself she often measured him against Phil Ward. Until Phil was gone, Agren could never be quite sure of the girl. There was envy of some subtle thing in Phil that Agren himself did not have—and he wouldn't admit that it was character. But Agren couldn't tell Reiger or a gunslinger like Dave Trego these things. He shrugged.

"I'm tired of seeing him lord around. I'd like to take over his contract. There're a dozen reasons."

"And one girl?" Trego asked softly. Agren flushed slightly and the gunman's sunken eyes glittered. "Ward is a damn hard man to corral."

Agren made an impatient gesture. "We've got to stop him quick and sudden."

"A big order." Trego walked to the door and leaned against the frame. Reiger and Agren sat silent, each evolving plans and as quickly rejecting them. Trego half turned and considered the two men at the table.

"Too bad Pennard didn't have time to stir up trouble among those construction stiffs. If—"

"That's it!" Agren shouted. Trego stared at him. Reiger's bullet head lifted and his muddy eyes looked blank. "Make 'em want to string him up to the nearest cottonwood limb."

"How?" Trego asked.

Agren chuckled. "Dave, suppose you worked six long days on that railroad and you looked forward to one day when you could forget it along with some whisky, gambling and a look at a woman? Then suppose you found out you don't get paid and you can't buy a damn thing—and suppose you learned that the boss was holding out?"

"I'd want to kill the boss," Trego said.

"There it is!" Agren exclaimed.

Trego sucked in his lean cheeks and his eyes glittered. "You mean steal Ward's payroll!"

"Exactly. The lost money would be something Ward can't replace very fast. He'd have to use funds he's got marked for supplies and equipment to cover the payroll, and it'd take him at least a week to arrange bank loans."

Trego stroked his bony chin. "Makes sense."

Agren swung to Reiger. "Milt, if your boys spread the word that Ward deliberately tried to steal their pay, what would happen?"

Trego chuckled. "Damn near anything."

Reiger grinned. "A hell of an idea, Hal! They'd string him up damn fast! How about it, Dave? Can you still handle a shotgun guard?"

"Do you ever forget, Milt?" he asked with a crooked grin. He looked at Agren. "Maybe you'd better mark out the trail a little better."

Agren told them that Phil Ward's payroll was brought in by stage from the east, a day ahead of payday. It was held at the local bank, where the actual pay envelopes were stuffed by clerks whom Phil sent over for that job. It was then taken to the construction camp and the workers were paid off on Saturday afternoon. Trego listened carefully, glanced at Reiger.

"I know just the place to hit the stage."

"How about the money?" Reiger demanded.

"Hell, Milt," Agren exclaimed impatiently, "we'll split it between us. The main thing is that we get Ward's men believing he's stealing the money and blaming it on a holdup."

Trego nodded. "We'd better wait until the camp is moved to Ensign."

"Why?"

"It'll make it easier for our boys to get the workers stirred up. Phil can't control the saloons in Ensign. If we time this just right, the whole thing will go off like clockwork."

They talked swiftly and eagerly, considering many angles, and at last hit upon a plan that would surely work. The conference broke up at last and the three men walked to their tethered horses. Hal swung into the saddle and lifted his hand in a salute.

"See you after the holdup."

He rode off. Reiger chuckled and touched the spurs lightly to his own mount. Trego rode beside him as they left the camp in a different direction. Trego glanced sidelong at Reiger, noticed his wide grin. Trego's dry voice cut through Reiger's pleasant thoughts.

"We'd better make damn sure this works, Milt."

"Why?" Reiger jerked out of his pleasant meanderings.

"If something should go wrong and this is blamed on you, I'd place even money you wouldn't live long. Phil Ward would be killing mad."

Reiger dismissed the warning. "It won't go wrong, Dave. You'll see to that. Ward wouldn't leave you out, either."

XVII

The days passed in a busy blur for Phil. There were, as always, a thousand and one details, but Phil saw the line of gleaming rails come closer and closer to Ensign. A mile a day was reached and maintained and the camp was moved without a hitch. Now the workers came nightly to Ensign, and this worried Phil. He did not have the control here that he did at end-of-track and he feared that the work reports would show a slackening. But on the contrary, the closer the rails came to town the more eagerly the men pushed them forward.

Nor was there any more trouble at the ranch. There had been no further sign of rustlers and Reiger's men carefully stayed some distance from the Flying W line. The ranch met its schedule. Beef drives for the construction camp circled the town.

There had to be close contact between the construction camp and the sawmill, but Phil let Tim Moriarty handle most of this, wanting little contact with Agren. The few times they chanced to meet on the street, Agren was cold and aloof, but always with a slight, knowing smile that infuriated Phil. It seemed to say that Agren knew Phil could never hope to reach Carol again. It was a bitter thought to know that Agren had won.

Phil tried to bury these hopeless thoughts in work. Fortunately, he did not see her, being in the office or out at the construction camp during those periods of the day when she shopped.

But he did see Fleming, who always talked to Phil with grave friendliness, but kept the conversation strictly on the railroad. Often Phil would catch Fleming covertly watching him with a strange, somber look in his eyes, but Fleming never spoke, seeming to tell himself that it was none of his business. Still, Phil felt that sooner or later Fleming would be bound to bring it up.

He was surprised when it did come, for Fleming had held his silence so long. The engineer had come into the office, cheerful about the progress reports. He, Tim and Phil conferred on some minor problems and Fleming complimented Tim on the way he had organized the work gangs. The big Irishman beamed.

"Sure, it was only part of the job."

"But you've done it well," Fleming insisted. "And you're due for praise, Phil. I wouldn't have taken odds you'd come out of it."

Phil smiled, then sobered. "If it hadn't been for men like Tim, I wouldn't have."

Fleming's smile vanished and the impulsive question burst from his lips. "Phil, what's wrong between you and Carol?"

Phil tried to keep his tone casual. "Nothing, Ray. I'm—just busy."

"That won't do, Phil. You never come around anymore and you keep me at a distance. I mention your name to Carol and she acts as though it put a bad taste in her mouth. She won't talk; maybe you will."

Phil looked out the office window, not knowing how to answer. Obviously Carol had told him nothing about the scene with Agren and there was no point in Phil's building up any more antagonism. He shrugged.

"It was a disagreement, Ray."

"Over Hal Agren?"

Phil saw no way out of it. "I guess that's about it."

"Outside of Hal, this thing between you and Carol is just a disagreement?"

"That's all," Phil said shortly.

Fleming slapped his hand on the chair arm. "If it's not important, I think you've both forgotten you're adults. Get your hat and come with me."

"Where?" Phil demanded.

Fleming was now on his feet, his jaw set. "To my house. We'll get this thing patched up right now."

Phil protested, but Fleming overrode him. Fleming wanted Carol to like Phil. She could be in love with Agren if she wanted, though Fleming implied he thought that was a mistake; but she did not have to treat Phil like an enemy.

Phil still argued but Fleming practically forced

him out of the office. Phil came close to telling him what had actually happened, but changed his mind. If Carol had not told her brother, why should Phil? If he did, Carol would never forgive him and he might even lose Fleming's respect.

They came to the house and Fleming led the way into the living room. He called Carol but there was no answer. He left Phil and returned in a few moments, a little crestfallen.

"I guess she's out shopping."

"Then I'll get back to the office," Phil said, relieved.

"No, you don't," Fleming snapped. "We'll wait." He started to sit down, looked at his hands and straightened. "I need to clean up. Make yourself comfortable."

He left before Phil could protest. Phil stood uncertainly by the table. He had an impulse simply to walk out, but he couldn't. He decided to wait for Fleming's return before he took himself out of this situation. The engineer would be back in a few moments.

The house was silent and Phil felt its uncomfortable pressure. He jumped up and picked his hat from the table, then the front door opened. There were light steps in the hall and he turned just as Carol stepped in, then stopped short with an exclamation of surprise. Carol's chin lifted defiantly.

"I hardly expected to find you here, Mr. Ward."

"Rayburn insisted I come."

"Rayburn?"

A door opened upstairs and Fleming's voice called. "Is that you, Carol? I'll be down as soon as I change. I want to get this thing between you and Phil settled. See if you two can be civilized a few moments."

She gasped and turned, her face blazing. "You've told him those unfounded suspicions about Hal."

"I've told him nothing," Phil answered shortly.

"You at least have the courtesy not to repeat the lie."

Phil's voice snapped like a lash. "I don't lie, Carol. I know what happened to me and I know who was behind it."

He strode to the table, his face paper-white and she met his look defiantly. Suddenly, he saw her as a beautiful woman, defending the man she loved, unwilling to listen to anything that would lessen his stature. He felt pity for her, and a sense of his own loss. It overwhelmed him so that he stepped close, his arms went swiftly about her.

Her eyes rounded and her mouth parted in surprise. Phil kissed her. For a second the stiffness went out of her body and her lips moved slightly beneath his, firm and yet soft.

The street door opened and Hal Agren stood immobile, staring. Carol suddenly stiffened, and her hands angrily shoved Phil back. She broke away, blazing angry. Agren took a furious step toward Phil.

"Get out!" he said between set teeth. Phil, shaken, looked from him to Carol. He took a deep breath, bowed deeply to Carol.

"I'm sorry," he said in a low voice. He turned on his heel and walked past Agren. His long strides carried him across the porch, down the steps and out the walk to the street. He hurried away, his thoughts a turmoil, wondering what had caused him to act as he had.

Back in the hall, Agren watched him go. Then he swung around, his handsome face suddenly ugly. Carol wiped a handkerchief across her lips, her eyes stormy.

Agren was still fighting anger but he smiled, a twisted move of the lips that was not pleasant to see. "I don't think you have to worry about Ward, since I'm going to see that he won't bother you much longer."

She looked up at his tone. "Hal, what are you going to do?"

"See that Mr. Ward is taken care of," he answered with easy assurance. He put his hands on her shoulders and his fingers pressed her flesh. His smile grew wider, strangely frightening. "I've already taken certain steps. Now he's gone too far. I'll just take one more. Mr. Ward won't stay long in Ensign—not after he's ruined."

His fingers gave her another pressure and he left

as abruptly as Phil had. Carol stood for a moment, and then hurried to the door. Hal was already at the end of the walk.

"Hal! What are you going to do!"

He turned, read the alarm on her face and waved airily. "I won't let anything happen to me, dear. I'm just going to see some friends who've been waiting to even a few scores themselves."

He walked away. Carol slowly moved to the swing and sank into it, face grave and puzzled. She still felt the pressure of Phil's lips on her own and she half raised her hand, but hastily dropped it. A deep color came into her cheeks and she felt again the lift of outrage and anger.

But her thoughts swung to Hal. She couldn't understand what he had implied. He had taken steps before this—and that had little meaning unless Hal had been fighting Phil in some way because of her. Apparently it had not been openly, to judge from the slyness in his tone.

She sank back, thoughtful and troubled, her hands in her lap. How would Hal fight Phil? She recalled Phil's accusation and she instantly rejected it. Yet her thoughts came back to it. Could it possibly be that Phil had been right? She shook her head. No, Hal wouldn't send a gunfighter to ambush a man! But then she found herself facing a question and she couldn't wholly answer.

Hal had his bad points and she felt that she

knew them. He needed to feel that. He was more important than anyone else. Agren boasted often without words but merely by his attitude toward things and people. She found herself reluctantly comparing the two men.

She had never heard Phil Ward boast about himself. He was quiet and seemed to get things done. He could move swiftly and strike hard, for Carol knew about the way he had cleaned up end-of-track. Would Hal be capable of that? She sighed, certain that he would not. Hal had many weak-nesses and he needed her because of them. But did that mean he would do as Phil accused him? And what did he plan now?

"Carol?"

She jumped and looked around. Rayburn stood in the doorway, puzzled.

"Did Phil leave?"

She licked her lips. "Yes."

Rayburn looked searchingly at her. "I thought I heard pretty angry sounds down here. Did he leave—"

"Angry?" she asked shortly. She stood up, her lips thinned. "Yes, he was angry."

She brushed by him and walked into the house. Fleming sensed something important here but he knew it would gain nothing to question her. He shrugged, and sank into the swing. He'd have to wait for another opportunity and then try again.

XVIII

The tempo of work picked up and entered the final hectic drive. The workers swung into it each morning, one work gang challenging another and all of them now eager to lay the rails into Ensign and start the long reach westward along the plateau toward the mountains and canyons between them and the Colorado River.

The grading crews approached the town and the tie and rail layers pushed hard behind them. Ensign itself was aware that within a few days it would be connected with the rest of the world. The mayor and city officials called on Phil, asking about the schedule and planning a celebration such as this town had never seen before. It was a pleasure to tell them that the rails should be in and through the town in ten days or less. They left to set the wheels in motion and Phil looked at Tim.

"Did you ever think this day would come?"

"There were times I knew it would not. And there is still work to be done, me lad."

That afternoon they went out to the camp with the payroll and Tim told the men what was planned for them in Ensign. The workers cheered and someone yelled in the crowd.

"We'll make it sooner."

"Do that!" Tim answered from the stack of ties

on which he stood. "But give 'em time to stretch the bunting across the street and finish the station."

"That's their worry," someone called. "We can walk back ten miles and attend the celebration."

Laughter ran through the crowd, which broke up to form lines before the various payclerks. Tim and Phil rode back to town, pleased.

The crews kept up the mile-a-day schedule. There was a new lift of spirit in the town, eager talk about the railroad, bets on when the rails would be spiked down before the newly painted station. The town officials made arrangements that the work train, the locomotive decorated with bunting and pulling two coaches instead of the usual flats, would pull into the station and stop before a platform to be built there. Telegrams were sent to railroad officials and the territorial governor. Important men were asked to ride the first train into Ensign.

Then, five days later, Phil was asked to come to the bank. Watterson handed him a telegram. Phil read it swiftly and looked up.

"Payroll delayed?"

Watterson nodded. "Once in a great while it happens. We can't carry cash enough to meet our own demands and that of your payroll. We arrange for the shipments from a bank in Albuquerque. The bank over there is caught in the same squeeze."

"The men won't like this," Phil said slowly.

"A two-day delay, that's all."

Phil's fingers drummed on the edge of the desk, then he shrugged. "I guess it can't be helped. I'll explain it to the men right away. It's not as if they've lost their pay."

"They'll understand that." Watterson arose and smiled. "Put the blame on us. Banks are used to being cussed out."

Phil returned to Tim's office and explained the situation. Tim didn't like it and looked worried.

"They're a rough bunch," Tim said, "and ye have to know how they'll think. They'll feel that they've given their work right on time, so they'll think that ye have not played fair with them."

Phil sat down at his desk, frowning. Suddenly his eyes lighted. "Two days, Tim. That's when Ensign plans its celebration. Tell 'em what's happened, then tell 'em first thing that morning they'll have all their wages in their pockets for the celebration. They'll have the day off, of course."

Tim smiled. "That might do it, me lad."

He grabbed his hat and was gone. He returned in the late afternoon and Phil looked for signs of trouble. Tim smiled widely.

"The job is done. Sure, at first they did not like it, but what man would not like a day off and his pockets filled with money?"

Phil was relieved. "You've done a good job, Tim."

The big Irishman sobered. "It had to be done. I

have seen the likes of them before when they lost their pay. It was not pretty."

"Well, this time we don't see it," Phil said and turned to the work on his desk.

The preparation for the celebration went ahead fast. Within a day the grading crews worked at the east end of town and many went out to watch them. The next day they pushed through the town and the dust clouds rose as they graded westward. Behind them came the ties and then the rails were placed, gauged and spiked.

Ensign prepared for the holiday. Red, white and blue bunting stretched across the main street and each store had crude signs welcoming the rails, the governor, prosperity. Word had spread through-out the surrounding territory and many of the ranches were sending in most of their men for the celebration. This would mark a historic day and no one wanted to miss it.

There were Navajos from the reservation and the ranches. They came riding proudly on their paint ponies, necks, arms and waists adorned with trade silver and turquoise, dark, impassive faces a strange contrast to the bright shirts and glittering jewelry.

Phil worried about the payroll. Tim and the foremen were alert for grumblings and they reported that there were a few, though that was to be expected. Phil was thankful that the workers' mood had not turned ugly. Tim, however, told him not to be too sure.

"I hear there is the whisper that ye have big bills and ye rob the workers to pay the others."

"How did that get started!"

"Sure, and ain't there always the spalpeens that'd put the wrong word to anything? We have told the truth where we've heard this. So far, they are content to wait the extra two days." Tim's wide forehead creased in a hundred wrinkles. "But if the payroll should not come, ye'd best be far away. A holiday and no pay—they'll be fighting mean."

Phil checked daily with the bank. Then Watterson greeted him one morning with a wide smile, waving a telegram.

"The money's on its way, Phil. It'll come by train from Albuquerque to Devil's Canyon station, then by coach under the usual guard."

"When will it get here?"

"You'll have it the day before the celebration."

Phil sighed in relief.

"I've worried about it," Watterson confessed, "and I've kept the telegraph busy."

Phil returned to the office with the good news. Until the work was completed to Ensign, the railroad had no scheduled run and the payroll might arrive at any time. Tim and Phil decided it would be best to ride out to the canyon on one of the work trains two days before the celebration. They would make sure the payroll arrived, and come back with it on the stagecoach.

"It would make ye feel better," Tim said. "And me, too, for that matter. 'Tis no good having to face a whole construction camp on a mad rampage. I have seen it, bucko."

They caught an empty work train and by midmorning they had breakfasted and waited for the west bound train at the small new station. It came in, a combination baggage coach, passenger car and three boxcars.

Phil and Tim hurried to the baggage car and were pleased to see the stout, padlocked iron box that contained the payroll. The stagecoach for the towns west of the canyon waited by the station and Phil helped transfer the strong box to the boot in the coach.

The driver climbed up to the seat, spoke to the shotgun guard and the horses lunged into their collars. The stage started with a jolt that threw Phil back against the inside seat. But he only smiled. There would be no trouble in Ensign now.

One of the loafers on the station platform sauntered to a saddled horse tethered nearby. The stranger swung into the saddle, and rode off westward at a long tangent to the road. Once out of sight of the town, the man cruelly set the spurs and his horse raced at top speed, steadily widening the distance between the rider and the coach that rolled along at a fast pace.

Within the coach, Phil and Tim eased into comfortable positions so that the jolts of the vehicle were lessened. There was a drummer and another guard sent by the bank in Albuquerque to augment the man who rode up above with the driver.

The steady roll of the coach, the rhythmic pounding of the horses' hoofs became lulling. Phil had slept only in snatches the night before and he was inclined to doze off. He caught himself several times. Each turn of the wheels brought the payroll closer to Ensign. There could surely be no trouble between here and the distant town. He roused briefly as the coach rattled over the long bridge that spanned Devil's Canyon. Just beyond, Phil saw the spidery structure of the railroad trestle.

The road curved and headed for a canyon that would take them through a series of broken hills. The steady pace of the coach slowed on the lifting grade and the changed rhythm of the hoofs awakened Phil. Tim sat on the opposite seat, head resting against the window frame, mouth hanging open and eyes closed. The drummer was smoking a cigar. The stage lurched around a curve, the road still climbing into the low pass between the hills. The canyon narrowed and the rocky walls pressed in on the road.

Rifles crashed without warning. A man yelled and a horse neighed as it went down. The others piled into it and the coach lurched sickeningly to one side, balanced a moment, and miraculously righted. Tim and the guard jerked awake, cursing. A shot sounded from the driver's seat and then the blast of a shotgun. Rifles blazed again and Phil heard a man's strangled scream.

His hand swept to his holster and jerked out the Colt. He threw the door open and instantly rifle bullets splintered the casing. Phil threw himself back, cursing. The drummer had dropped flat on the floor and his body was an obstruction. Tim stumbled over him trying to reach the other door. The drummer covered his head in his arms and moaned.

The bank guard jerked open the door and jumped out, Colt in his hand. He looked about, seeking the ambushers. He never had a chance. He whipped about as slugs struck him. His gun flew from his hand in a glittering arc and he fell back against the stage.

The horses fought the tangled harness and the coach jerked erratically. Tim and Phil crouched in the open windows, guns ready. Phil caught the glint of a movement up on the rim of the cliffs and he threw a quick shot upward. He saw dust jump from the edge of the cliff and knew he had undershot. The driver's body suddenly toppled by the window.

Tim fired three times in quick succession, his face drawn and tight, lips pulled savagely back over his teeth. More bullets sought them and long splinters jumped along the edge of the seat. The drummer suddenly jerked spasmodically, a scream choking off as he fell back on the floor and didn't move.

"We've got to get out of here," Phil shouted. Tim curtly signaled over his shoulder to the other door.

"Rocks are closer on that side. I'll hold them here while you make a run. Then you cover me."

Phil clambered over the drummer's body as Tim systematically fired up toward the cliff rim. Phil peered out, searching for possible cover. Tim's steady fire had drawn the attention of the bushwhackers to that side of the coach. Phil saw a little side canyon, hardly more than a crevice, a few yards away. If he and Tim could make it, they might have a temporary haven. He moved back to Tim's side and told what he planned.

Tim ejected empties from his Colt and grimly nodded. Phil returned to the other side, cautiously pushed the door wider. No bullets sought him out and Tim's gun was a constant roar and flash. Phil jumped outside.

He ran, crouching, toward the narrow crack in the canyon wall. Instantly bullets winged past him. Some kicked dust close and others whined spitefully beside his ears. He strained forward, legs pumping. Another bullet whipped close to his head, and then the shadows of the narrow walls closed about him. He was safe.

He whirled about, searching across the main canyon. Two of the horses were down, either killed or badly wounded, and the others were hopelessly entangled. The stage still jerked back and forth as the horses tried to lunge free. The shotgun guard was sprawled on top of the coach.

Tim's gun thundered steadily and was answered from the rim across the canyon. The ambushers had picked a perfect place for their job. Phil edged forward to the mouth of the canyon and crouched behind a boulder. Face set, he placed bullets along the far rim, aiming for the gun flashes.

The firing up there instantly slacked off. It died completely for a moment and then suddenly reopened in new fury, every bullet slapping onto the big rock that protected Phil. He heard the constant high whine of the ricochets. He replied as best he could.

Tim emerged from the coach and Phil wondered how the bushwhackers could miss so large a target. His lips set and he slammed shots against the far rim with a reckless abandon. Tim raced toward him, moving with amazing speed for so heavy a man. Phil saw dust gout close to the huge booted feet. Suddenly a man rose in sight on the far rim, forgetting himself in his anxiety to get the fleeing Irishman. Phil instantly centered his gun as the man leveled a rifle. Phil did not hurry his shot, making sure, and his finger slowly squeezed the trigger.

The man on the rim spun about as Phil's gun bucked. The bandit balanced on the rim and then abruptly plunged downward. He sprawled at the foot of the cliff, just beyond the coach. Phil had a glimpse of the slack face and jerked with surprise. That was the man who had helped Braxton at end-of-track, one of Joe Pennard's gunhawks.

Tim lunged by Phil into the safety of the narrow canyon. Bullets still struck the rock. Tim sank to the ground. His barrel chest heaved and sweat streamed from his face. Phil answered the bandits until their firing slacked off. Tim touched his sleeve.

"It's best we get out of here, bucko." He pointed upward. "It will be no trouble for them to work around to this side and they'd have us down here like snakes in a barrel."

"You're right," Phil snapped.

Tim angrily looked at the stage. "But there is the payroll."

"Can't be helped," Phil said flatly.

Tim cursed under his breath, knowing there was nothing they could do. Phil threw more shots at the opposite rim, then nodded to Tim and beat a quick retreat down the narrow canyon.

Tim puffed and cursed behind him. The narrow space twisted and turned until Phil began to wonder if it would be a death trap. It suddenly widened and Phil saw a shallow cave halfway up a steep slope. He wasted no breath, but simply pointed. Tim nodded and followed him.

They scrambled upward, panting and sweating. At last they sank down within the mouth of the cave. Now they could not be picked off from above and the only approach was directly up the slope where their own guns could hardly miss. They could hold off a hundred bandits in this stronghold.

They waited, tense. They heard a faint shout once, but at no time did they see any pursuers. The sun moved serenely westward. Once Phil moved impatiently toward the mouth of the cave, but Tim pulled him back.

"*Whsst,* and would ye have all our run for nothing! Just one man out there could bring ye down. Best wait."

"How long?" Phil exclaimed. "Until they starve us out?"

"No," Tim said slowly and his eyes darkened. "Only until they have the payroll and have ridden off. It's the money they want, not our scalps."

He was right. Phil turned his thoughts to the loss of the payroll, a paralyzing blow. If it was not recovered, he could be put out of business, unless he was first hanged by irate workers. He looked bleakly out on the silent, impassive canyon, his thoughts moving in futile circles. At last he could stand the waiting no longer and he came to his feet.

"I'm going back," he said.

Tim hitched at his gunbelt. "It might be safe now."

They moved to the mouth of the cave and searched that part of the canyon walls that they could see. Nothing moved. Phil glanced at Tim.

"Here goes."

He stepped out, ready for trouble, Tim following him. Nothing happened. They moved cautiously down the canyon, but there was only the silence of the hills about them. They carefully approached the mouth of the side canyon.

The stave still stood where they had last seen it. The horses had stopped fighting the tangled harness and now stood patiently. The shotgun guard still lay atop the coach, the driver and bank guard sprawled where they had fallen. The scars of the bullets looked fresh and raw. Phil searched the rimrock, but there was no sign of the ambushers. The fallen bandit no longer lay at the foot of the wall. Tim slowly straightened.

"They're gone."

"Let's look at the coach," Phil said tightly.

The drummer lay on the floor, his glassy eyes staring. The boot had been ransacked and the strongbox lay on the ground, the lock blasted open. It was empty.

Tim looked up at Phil. "This will be a bad bit of news at the camp."

Phil's jaw set. He didn't reply, but circled the stage to the horses. He cut away the harness and

Tim helped him. They finally released the horses and each mounted one. Phil pointed to the trail the bandits had left and they moved down the canyon, westward. Phil was certain the outlaws would not leave clear sign and, sure enough, it vanished where the canyon debouched onto the plain beyond. Off to the right, the glitter of the new rails mocked Phil.

"They're gone," Tim said, indicating the trail. Phil nodded. From this point the outlaws could have ridden in any direction. Tim sighed. "Ye'll not see hide nor hair of them again . . . nor of your money."

"I'm not so sure," Phil said. He told about the man he had shot. Tim's blue eyes widened.

"Joe Pennard! But ye run him out of town!"

"Maybe he left, maybe not. Maybe he joined up with the outlaws on his own; maybe it was orders. But I've got a lead to the outlaws."

"Who would they be?" Tim demanded.

Phil lifted the reins. "Let's get to Ensign. If we've got time enough left, we might get the payroll back. If we haven't—"

He left it unsaid and Tim knew what he meant. Joe Pennard, Phil thought. That means Reiger is back of this and, if he and Trego engineered this, then Hal Agren must be in the shadows.

It was time for a showdown—if Phil could bring it about before hell broke loose in the construction camp.

XIX

They came to Ensign about twilight, tired, grim and discouraged. The gay bunting and the excited crowds seemed to mock them. Phil headed directly to the office, and Tim looked surprised.

"If too many people see us riding these coach horses," Phil said shortly, "there'll be questions."

They reached the office without interruption. Phil walked to the sheriff's office while Tim headed for the stage station, to tell the manager to keep the news quiet until the lawman could take charge.

Jere Miles listened in dismay as Phil told him what had happened. He immediately arose to collect a posse, but Phil stopped him.

"We've got to keep it quiet, Miles. Can your posse slip out of town?"

"Sure, but you can't keep a thing like this under cover, Phil."

"No one knew the payroll was coming on this stage."

"Now, wait," Miles lifted his hand. "Someone knew, or they wouldn't have held it up."

Phil's smile was no more than a pulling of the lips back from the teeth. "I know that, Miles, and they're the ones I must find. I must have the chance to recover that payroll before the word leaks out."

Miles slowly nodded. "I can savvy that. You could have some trouble with your boys."

"That's a nice way of saying it, Miles. Get your posse together quietly. The news will leak out, of course, but say nothing about the payroll. I'll try to pick up leads in town. Maybe together, we'll get it back."

The sheriff was discreet. Word spread that the stage had been hit by outlaws, but nothing was said about the payroll. The exciting news only added spice to the town's celebration. After the posse left, Phil and Tim returned to the construction office.

"And now what would ye be doing?" Tim asked.

"Pick up Pennard's trail. Find out what Reiger and Trego have been doing the last few days."

"Ye've set yourself a job."

"I know it. And you, too, Tim. We've got to search the saloons tonight and watch the crowds. Look for Pennard, or anyone who used to be with him. Watch for Trego or any of the Lazy R hands. If they're in this deal, they might talk at the bars. Listen. Maybe we'll get a line."

"Why not find Milt Reiger?" Tim demanded.

Phil grinned crookedly. "Reiger knows I'm suspicious of him. He stayed far away from that holdup, and probably has witnesses to prove it. We have to find some of the lesser breed and work our way to Reiger—and the payroll."

"And ye can pray that they have not divided the money and it is scattered."

"I am."

Phil went home, washed and changed clothes. He wished he could shed his worry as easily, but he strapped on his gunbelt and checked the Colt. He forced himself to eat a meal, knowing that the night's celebration was not yet in full swing. The outlaws would not feel safe enough to appear in the bars until later.

Finally Phil went out on the streets. He had tonight, tomorrow and the next night in which to recover the payroll. If the morning of the official welcoming of the railroad came and his men were not paid . . .

Every saloon was crowded, each bar lined two and three deep. Phil moved steadily from one place to another, eyes constantly searching. He asked discreet questions, but by midnight he had learned nothing. He met Tim at one of the saloons and the Irishman's expression was discouraged.

They went outside and found a secluded place between two buildings where they could compare notes. Tim had no line on Pennard, or on any of the gun-slammers and bouncers who had worked for him.

"But he's around somewhere," Phil said tightly. "That was his man I shot."

"There're a thousand places he could hide," Tim said.

"Seen any of Reiger's men?" Phil asked.

Tim shook his head. "I have not. Word has spread the stage was held up."

"Any talk about the payroll?"

"None, though I heard a gandy dancer say it was lucky his money was not among the loot."

Phil wearily passed his hand over his face. "We still have a chance, though time's running out. Let's try again."

The night passed with no lead. Just before dawn Phil wearily undressed and threw himself on his bed. He was so tired and worried that he lay tense and knotted for some time before he drifted off into a broken sleep. He awoke feeling as though he had been beaten with clubs during the brief three hours that he had managed to sleep. He had breakfast and went to Tim's office.

Tim had found no trace of Reiger's men or of Pennard. Phil went over the reports on the desk and Tim stopped on his way out to the construction camp. He looked worried, uncertain what to say, and Phil glanced up to catch the shadows in Tim's eyes.

"Is it that bad?" he asked, dropping the reports.

"There is just today . . . and tonight."

"I know."

Tim started to say something more, changed his mind and reluctantly walked out of the office. Phil stared at the bright morning sunshine streaming through the windows. Just today and tonight! He could not possibly meet the payroll. If Reiger and Agren were behind this, they had hit him hard.

He went out to the street with a feeling of hopelessness that he couldn't shake. Only a dogged determination kept him going from place to place where he would meet men who might give him that first, faint lead.

Tim found him in one of the saloons and Phil wondered what had brought the man from the camp. Tim came up to the bar, and indicated that he would like to see Phil at the office. Something in his face made Phil swing away and walk out with him. In the office, Tim wasted no time.

"Word's getting around the payroll was mixed up in that robbery, Phil."

"How did it leak?"

"I don't know, and that is not the point. It is also whispered that ye have been pressed for money and that ye use this holdup to cheat the men to meet your other bills."

Phil stared at him, aghast. "Who said that?"

"I don't know where it started. The men are getting mad."

"But—"

Tim's lifted hand stopped Phil's protest. "There is more and it is ugly. There is also talk that they should ask for their pay. If ye cannot produce it, then 'tis proof that ye intend to cheat them. If that is so, then ye should be strung up to the nearest tree."

Phil's jaw tightened. "I think it's time I told you about Agren and Reiger."

"Hal Agren!"

Phil nodded and then told Tim of what Braxton said just before he died, of the way Agren had confirmed his guilt by his own actions. Phil wryly spoke of Carol Fleming and her defense of Agren and of the incident at the Fleming home. Tim listened, his jaw dropping. He gave a long whistle.

"Ye make an ugly picture, bucko. I never did take to Hal Agren, but I would not have read such a black heart in the likes of him." His thick fingers tapped on the desk. "If it is true that Agren and Reiger wish to be rid of ye, then they're close to it this day."

"And getting closer," Phil said. "We have only until tomorrow morning."

Late that afternoon Carol watched Hal Agren turn in at the walk. She met him at the door, kissed him lightly on the cheek. He looked at her with mock severity.

"And is that all the kiss you have for me?"

She laughed as she turned back in the house. "What have you done to deserve more?"

He shrugged and she thought he had been about to say something but had changed his mind. There had been a fleeting firming of his jaw, a

228

swift set of his lips into something harsh and cruel, and then it was gone.

"A big day, and a heavy one."

"Then you should be pleased with the mill's business."

Again she thought he started to tell her something. He followed her to the kitchen where she was preparing pastries for supper. He sat down at the table and watched her deft, sure hands. Now and then she threw a swift, covert glance at him. He was obviously pleased with himself for some secret reason. There was something smug about him, as though he had pulled off some very clever deal.

She had never encountered quite this attitude before. Rayburn had sometimes been pleased. He had met a problem—a mountain to be skirted or tunneled, a hill that tended to slide, and his own engineering skill had curbed it. But Hal's was something different. Then she had it. Rayburn's pleasure was that of a man who met an antagonist head on, pitting his knowledge, skill and power as one soldier would against another. But Hal's was like that of a man who has consummated a sharp deal and his opponent has not yet realized it, of a man who has pulled a trick and is smug. Her mind posed a new and troubling thought.

"You know this is the way he is . . . the way he will always be. Are you willing to accept it?"

These questions had become important since that tumultuous moment when Phil Ward, in his anger, had kissed her. Even now, with Hal sitting at the table, she knew a sharp, secret warmth at the memory of it and she wondered at her inconsistency.

Faintly, through the open window, there came the sound of the crowd on the main street. Perhaps a shift of the wind had brought it. Hal lifted his head and Carol paused in her work. She smiled.

"Ensign's glad to get a railroad."

Hal laughed. "And I brought it to them, Carol."

She couldn't help her frown. "That's true, Hal . . . you and the men in your camps, all the workers at your mill, all the gandy dancers who work for Phil."

She realized her slip in her familiar use of his name. Agren stirred restlessly and she knew that he had some faint inkling of her thoughts. She braced for his reply. But they both turned when the front door banged and Rayburn's quick, heavy steps sounded down the hall. He looked in at them.

"You're back early," Carol said. He nodded, standing indecisively in the doorway.

"The work on the road has stopped."

"Stopped?" Carol exclaimed. "But the holiday's not until tomorrow!"

"The men left the job. They heard the payroll was lost in that stagecoach robbery—"

"The sheriff said nothing about it," Agren cut in. Fleming gave him a sharp glance.

"That's the trouble. The workers don't believe it

230

was stolen. They've heard Phil plans to cheat them out of it."

"Phil wouldn't do a thing like that!" Carol exclaimed.

"We know it," Fleming agreed, "but the men don't. There's some pretty wild talk about beating it out of him, or hanging him."

"Oh, no!" Carol whispered.

"It might have happened that way," Agren said quietly.

Fleming slapped the door frame with his open palm. "I know Ward better than that. I'll try to find him before anything serious happens. I could use your help, Hal."

Agren started, then caught himself. "I'll be along."

Fleming nodded and walked down the hall. They heard him climb the stairs and there were faint sounds from above. He appeared in the door-way again, a gunbelt strapped about his waist.

"Coming, Hal?"

"In a few minutes, Ray."

He turned after Fleming had left and saw that Carol was obviously worried. He considered her from under his brows and then studied his fingers.

"I wonder if Ward *did* use the payroll for something else. It would be like him."

"Hal!"

He flushed angrily. "You're mightily concerned about him."

"They might lynch him, Hal! Doesn't that mean anything to you?"

"Very little," he said shortly. "I don't see why I should worry about him. Anyway, he'll soon be out of the picture."

She searched his face. His eyes met hers, then wavered and slipped away. She remembered what Phil had said at the sawmill office and now, looking back, she realized that everything had rung true. Hal had made no real effort to deny the accusation, but he had evaded it and she remembered now that he had been happy to allow her to defend him. A spate of horrible thoughts came flooding in. She blurted the words before she could check them.

"Hal, you're behind this. That's why you know he'll be out of the picture!"

She saw the guilty expression on his face, and her horror grew. She had accidentally uncovered the truth and Hal could not hide his consternation. Her face blanched.

"It's true, Hal. You're inciting those men to hurt Phil, maybe hang him! What kind of a man are you?"

She circled the table in her agitation and stood over him. He involuntarily shrank back and his eyes shifted about. He didn't arise indignantly in honest anger. He can't, she thought—because he *has* done this thing. She felt as though she looked upon something evil that she had believed to be good.

"Hal, why? Do you hate Phil Ward so much you'd stoop to murder or mob violence! Do you actually want to see him hanged!"

Agren realized that he had not reacted swiftly enough and the delay had disclosed the whole scheme. He could not persuade her otherwise; denial would only make it worse. He must excuse himself in the one way that any woman would understand. He moistened his lips and his eyes narrowed. She did not miss the slight movement.

"Carol, I . . ." He sought for words. "I've carried this too far, perhaps. But I'm crazy in love with you. I was afraid Phil Ward might take you from me."

"But I loved you!"

He made a swift gesture. "I know, Carol. But he always tried. He accused me of many things, trying to ruin my character."

"He told the truth."

"He lied!" Agren said, but his eyes told another story, and again she felt that horrible physical uneasiness. He arose. "I want you all to myself, Carol. I can have you no other way. Ward has always tried to shake you from me and I saw this chance to stop him permanently. I thought if he was out of the way, I could have our love safe and forever, and perhaps Rayburn would let me take over—"

"Hal!" The utter loathing in the single word brought him up short. He really saw her for the first time. It was only right that he should destroy a love rival as he would a business opponent. He should also profit from the deal if he could. Her horror astounded him. She could not envision such a thing, and it angered him.

"For God's sake, Carol, grow up! These things are done every day. Maybe not in just this way, but—"

Her nostrils pinched. Anger, betrayal, torture, contempt showed in her eyes, and that was like a lash to Hal's ego. He grabbed her shoulders.

"Who are you for . . . him or me? Whom do you love . . . him or me? Have I done so wrong that—"

"You've done a horrible and despicable thing, Hal Agren. You're a sneak and a killer. How can I ever trust you or love you!"

"Then you don't?"

"We're through, Hal," she said in sudden quietness. "If you'd do this to Phil—"

He stood drawn and taut. His eyes blazed and his mobile lips worked in anger. He lifted his hand and she involuntarily shrank back. His face suffused and darkened.

"You're quite sure, Carol?" he asked just as quietly.

"Quite sure."

He walked to the door, stopped, and turned. His voice seemed to hiss and his nose and mouth were drawn.

"I told Rayburn I'd help him. Now I won't turn

a hand if they try to string Phil Ward up. You can thank yourself for that." He left and the house echoed silence as Carol stood tense and stunned.

Agren hurried down the street. He was still buffeted by wild, seething anger and jealousy. It lengthened his stride, arms taut, his fists clenched until the knuckles showed white. In some way Phil Ward had bested him at the last moment and he must be made to pay for this victory. Agren still had no idea that his own actions and words had betrayed him.

He swung around the corner into the main street. Bunting made gay splashes of color that he did not notice. Men spoke in voices that made no impression. He angrily shoved his way through the batwings of the nearest saloon and pushed to the bar, ordered his drink and tossed it down.

The bite of the whisky gave him a false balance, a pseudo awareness of what went on. He realized that three railroad laborers stood near, speaking angrily and loudly. Beyond them he saw a man of the type Reiger had on his payroll. The man smiled crookedly when one of the workers banged his fist on the bar.

"By God! Why should our money go to buy his fine clothes or pay his debts! I've swung a pick ten hours a day, six days a week. I've sweated and strained for the damn little dinero that I get. He ain't gonna gyp me."

"But what'll we do, Bill?" another asked.

"I say make him pay. If he don't, I reckon there's enough of us and plenty of rope in the town. It'll be the last time he'll cheat honest workmen!"

The puncher nodded. "I like to hear men with spunk. Not many would have your guts, mister."

"Oh, I can stand up for my rights," Bill said. He swung to the other two. "Let's find some of the other boys . . . see what they think."

They shoved away from the bar. Agren felt a tight lift of triumph. If this kept up— He hurried outside and caught the puncher as he started to leave with the workers. A swift question and as swift an answer sent Agren striding down the street once more.

He turned into another saloon, crowded as the rest. He did not see Reiger or Trego, but a gambler pointed to the wooden balcony when Agren asked about the men. Agren almost ran up the stairs, opened the door of one of the private rooms. Reiger and Trego sat at a table, a whisky bottle between them, intent on a game of cribbage. Trego looked up, right hand moving to the edge of the table. His cavernous eyes glinted.

"Ain't you running a chance of being seen with us?" he asked. Agren disregarded the sarcasm. He whipped a chair out from under the table.

Reiger grinned. "What's all the excitement,

Hal? It's all going exactly as we figured it would."

"It's got to go faster. Fleming's trying to find Ward right now and hide him."

Reiger considered this, while Agren glanced nervously at Trego. Finally Reiger shrugged.

"Hell, don't worry about that! He can't get the money where we've got it hid. He can't show his face in town or they'll hang him. He won't have a man working for him by morning—even if he's still alive. There goes his contract and everything else. We step in and it's all over."

Agren's fist banged on the table. "It's not enough."

"You sure as hell want his scalp," Trego said in surprise. "You still afraid of him with that girl of yours?"

Agren swung toward him, half lifting from his seat. Something in Trego's deep-set, steady eyes was like a rattler's warning and Agren sank back again.

"What's the difference?" He looked to Reiger. "You know, Pennard's man was killed out there. Maybe Ward recognized him. Suppose he finds Joe? Then where will you and I be?"

Reiger shook his head. "There's damn little chance. He'll be killed first. We'll keep stirring things up."

"Good," Agren said. "I'll do some stirring on my own. Meet you here in half an hour?"

"Any time," Reiger said affably and glanced at

Trego. "Dave, maybe you'd better spur the boys a little. We got to have us a sudden hanging or our new partner will be mighty unhappy."

Agren glowered but hurried out. He stood on the balcony looking on the milling men below. He wondered who could stand against them if they were suddenly stirred to violence. It would sweep Phil Ward out of existence. He hurried down the stairs.

A strange sort of fever drove him. Things were not quite real and yet he saw everything clearly, heard things clearly, knew what he did when he gathered several of his men at the sawmill. These were men whom he had long ago decided would do anything for money. They had a propensity for trouble, a facet of their characters that seemed an echo of his own.

"No point in you working when the rest of the town is drinking it up. I think you deserve a vacation." He pulled a thick roll of bills from his pocket and gave them a few seconds to eye it. "But you might do something for me."

"Sure, Hal," one of them said instantly, eyes still on the money. "Anything."

"Have your drinks on me," Hal said generously. "The railroad workers are in town; you'll meet 'em everywhere. They're mad clean through. Phil Ward has stolen their pay. I don't like that—" He paused. "I don't like Phil Ward. Maybe you don't either."

One of the sawyers spoke up. "If someone stole my pay, I'd be mad enough to hang him, I reckon."

Agren looked levelly at the man and then the others. He peeled off bills and distributed them.

"See what you can do about it," he said.

They accepted the money. Agren watched them walk down the slope to the main street. Reiger's renegades already spread rumors, whispers and incendiary thoughts, and these men would add to them. Agren's lips moved in a harsh grimace. Maybe Carol was lost, but Phil Ward would not live long enough to know it. With Phil gone, Carol might realize her error.

For more than an hour Carol restlessly paced the house, horrified at what Agren had disclosed. At first she could only think of this in relation to herself. She had found the most precious thing in the world shoddy and evil, twisted beyond recognition. She asked herself time and again how a man so handsome, apparently so kind and thoughtful, could coldly and deliberately plan murder.

She cried, then realized that this changed nothing. She must face the fact that Agren was beyond the help of any person. She would only throw herself away if she married him. She clearly recalled little things about Phil Ward, his refusal to push himself forward, his quiet surety.

She remembered now the way Phil silently watched her, worship in his eyes, and she recalled the feel of his lips on hers.

She had come to Hal's defense, so swiftly and forcefully that Phil never had a chance to tell her the reasons for his accusations. She had condemned him out of hand and had called it all a lie. What a fool she had been!

What a fool she was now! She brought herself up short. She remained here bewailing her own loss when out in the town, perhaps this very moment, an angry mob sought to kill Phil Ward. Her eyes widened with the shock of the thought. Rayburn wasn't here, so he could not help. She fled down the hall and out onto the street. The moment she turned the corner into the main street, the crowd engulfed her. She had to force her way through it. Men gave way to this beautiful woman with the distraught eyes who frantically elbowed by them. She sought vainly for Phil, her brother, or even Tim Moriarty. A drunk grabbed her and wheeled her around. Instantly a man stepped forward and shoved the drunk aside. Carol hurried on, the whole thing but a small fragment of a larger nightmare.

She approached one of the larger saloons as the batwings exploded outward and angry men streamed out. The crowd surged back and Carol was caught in the press, unable to move. The men rushed into the street yelling, and she was but hazily aware that they were construction workers. Then the comment of someone close by shocked her into awareness, and a cold horror and fear.

"The sheriff won't be able to stop that bunch. They'll hang Phil Ward or wreck the town."

Carol looked at them in horror, then blindly pushed her way back through the crowd. She broke free and looked distractedly about. If she could work her way around the mob she might find Phil before it was too late. She saw a narrow passage between a saddle shop and photographer's studio and she darted into it.

The alley was clear and she ran along it, judging by the roaring sound from the street that she had passed the mob. From the increasing volume of the ugly sound, she knew that it had picked up many more as it streamed along in search of its victim. Carol increased her speed, her breath coming fast and hard.

She passed two side streets, turned up the third to the main street again. Reaching the corner, she threw a frightened glance back toward the mob. It still milled in the street front of a hardware store. Fear clutched at her throat. Some of them had gone inside for hemp rope while the rest waited impatiently.

A step sounded behind her and she whirled. Her jaw dropped in consternation. Phil Ward stood there, puzzled and worried. His face was drawn and grim.

"Phil!" Her voice sounded strange. "Run! They want to hang you!"

"I know," he said.

"It was Hal—all the time. I just found it out," she babbled. "Oh, Phil, I've been so wrong! I didn't believe you. I—just couldn't."

"I understand," he said in sudden gentleness. His hands abruptly grasped her shoulders and he kissed her, swiftly.

"I've just learned where Reiger and Trego are hiding," he said quickly. "They got the payroll, and I think I can save it."

"They'll kill you!"

"It's better than a rope, anyhow. Get back home, Carol. I'll see you there when this is over."

He swung her about to lead her back to the alley. Suddenly there was a surprised shout close by. Phil whirled. Across the street, a group of construction workers had emerged from a small saloon.

"There he is!" a man shouted.

"Hurry!" Phil said.

Carol ran with him to the alley hearing angry shouts behind her, the pound of boots. A gun blasted but the shot went wild and high. They whipped about the corner into the empty alleyway. A second later the main mob swept into view from the other street and raced toward them. They were trapped.

XX

Phil and Carol stood poised and immobile as the two groups descended upon them. Then Phil whirled her about and pushed her toward the buildings and the temporary haven of a space between them. The howl of the mob lifted triumphantly.

They reached the narrow confine and Carol saw that on the far end it was blocked by a high fence. Phil turned to meet the mob and his hand swept his Colt out of the holster. Carol was never quite clear afterwards why she stepped up to Phil and, as the howling mob raced into view, pushed him behind her.

"Run! I'll hold them! They won't harm a woman!"

She took a step beyond the passage. It was totally unexpected. The mob found its way blocked by a slender, white-faced girl. The men halted and milled.

Phil stood tense and stunned. He realized that Carol faced the mob to give him a final, slim chance of recovering the money and redeeming himself. His impulse was to sweep her aside and face those men in her stead. But he knew that Carol would never forget that he threw himself away after she had done so much. It was no time for useless heroics. He ran down the passage and jumped to the top of the fence and over it. He heard the uncertain growl of the mob and knew that Carol still held them. He threw a hasty glance up and down the empty street. The saloon where he knew Reiger waited was in the next block. Phil raced for it.

There was no sound of pursuit. He breathed a grim prayer of thanks to Carol but knew that time rapidly ran out. The mob would swing out of the alley and into the street, searching for him.

He reached the saloon, raced through the bat-wings. Except for the bartender, the place was empty. The man stared as though he saw a ghost and stepped hastily back when Phil vaulted the bar and grabbed his shirt front.

"Where's Milt Reiger?"

"I—don't know."

"I've no time to waste," Phil snapped and shoved his Colt in the man's paunch. "Where's Reiger?"

"Up there—second door." The bartender indicated the balcony with his eyes. Phil wheeled the man around and propelled him toward a storage room in the rear. He went without argument or alarm. Phil closed the door and dropped the open lock in the hasp.

He wheeled about. He could hear the rumble of the mob. It had swept out into the main street and it would search him out, he knew. Jaw set, he hastened up the stairs and approached the closed door on the balls of his feet, making no sound.

He leveled the gun, and then opened the door, stepping inside. Four men were seated at the big table in the center of the room. Phil glimpsed Agren's pale face, Pennard's sudden start. Reiger's broad back was to him, but Dave Trego's skull features did not change expression when he looked up.

"I've been looking for you," Phil said tightly. "Don't move. I don't have a thing to lose."

Agren swallowed hard, and Pennard's sallow face broke out in a sweat. Reiger's hands remained flat on the table. Trego's head turned slightly as Phil came into the room, gun leveled, hammer dogged back.

Pennard flinched uncontrollably and Phil's gun swung to him. Trego took advantage of the slight break. There was only a blur of movement and the man's gun muzzle appeared over the edge of the table. Phil caught the glint of it and threw himself to one side. His Colt jerked about and he pulled the trigger. Two long lances of flame jumped toward one another. Trego tipped backward and disappeared.

Reiger moved and Phil swung toward him. He heard a man's yell of fright but his attention was centered on the renegade rancher whom he could dimly see through the cloud of gunsmoke. Reiger fired first, sweeping out his gun while Phil still faced Trego. The rancher slammed a shot before the gun was leveled and the bullet whipped above Phil's head to smash into the wall. Phil was in a crouch and he fired two fast shots at the big rancher. Someone crashed into him, sending him sprawling just as Reiger fired again. There was a choked cry of terror and a figure sprawled beside Phil.

He desperately pushed it aside and threw another shot at the rancher. The big man came up on his toes, his gun spilling from his hand. He crashed across the table. It tipped, balanced crazily and then fell to the floor, Reiger's limp body rolling from it.

Phil whipped about, but there were no more guns to face. Trego's bony form lay beyond the table in the limp sprawl of death. Reiger's chest was a mass of blood and he didn't breathe. The figure lying beside Phil made whimpering sounds of pain and fright.

He came to his feet and rolled the man over. Joe Pennard had been hit in the arm, but his eyes had the glazed appearance of fright and panic. Hal Agren was not in the room and Phil could see him racing to bring the mob.

He shook Pennard until some semblance of sanity came back in the muddy eyes. Phil shoved the Colt muzzle under the man's nose and dogged back the hammer.

"You've got three seconds to talk or take a bullet," he grated.

Pennard's breath came in swift, choking gasps, and he spoke in a strangled voice. He shrank from Phil, who never released his grasp of the man's shirt front. Joe saw no pity in the harsh, level eyes.

Joe blurted the whole story. He knew, from what Reiger and Trego had said, what part Agren had taken in the affair, how he had been pulled in beyond retreat by his unfounded jealousy and his overweening desire to make his fortune, no matter who would be hurt.

"The robbery," Phil snapped.

"Reiger and Agren planned it. Trego carried it off. Some of my boys took a hand."

"Where's the money?" Phil demanded.

"Hidden—sawdust pile at Agren's mill. We intended to split it once you—were out of the way."

Phil jerked the man to his feet and shoved him toward the door. The saloon was still empty, but Phil knew he had only minutes. It would be touch and go now—and he still might dangle from the end of a rope. He could see the way out if he could only reach it.

He shoved Pennard, unresisting, down the stairs and into a passage that opened on the empty alley. A rising sound from the street told him that the mob approached the saloon, probably led by Hal Agren. Phil cast over several possible routes, rejecting some, knowing that he dared not appear on the street or at Tim Moriarty's office.

Fleming's railroad office was not far away, and it would be unlikely that the mob would look for him there. It was a gamble, but it must be taken. Phil shoved Pennard ahead and they moved swiftly away from the saloon. There were some tense, bad moments at two street crossings. Phil expected the shout of discovery behind him, but they finally came unseen to the railroad office. Phil hustled Pennard into the door.

Fleming and Jere Miles wheeled around. Both men shoved cartridges in the loops of gunbelts, obviously planning to try to stop the mob. Their jaws dropped when they saw Phil.

"For God's sake!" Fleming exclaimed. "Get out of town, Phil, before they—"

"No time. Joe, tell them what it's all about."

Pennard again told his story. Fleming and Miles listened, amazement and disgust in their eyes as Pennard's story unrolled. At last Pennard finished and Fleming looked at the sheriff.

"Miles, you stay with Phil and this sidewinder. I'll find Tim Moriarty and we'll get that payroll money."

"I'll go—" Phil started but Fleming interrupted.

"You'll stay right here, Phil. We'll get that money and pay off the men. Until then, you stay under cover."

"Agren?"

"I'll take care of Agren," Miles said tightly, "once I've got you out of danger. Robbery, murder and inciting to violence will hold that bright young boy where he belongs for a long time."

Fleming left and there was nothing to do but wait. Twice the roar of the searching mob sounded close, then faded away. Time passed and Phil wondered what could be happening. Pennard sat in a corner, shaken and sullen. Miles waited by the office window, impassive and patient. Phil could only pace back and forth, worried about Fleming, more worried about Carol and feeling a rush of deep respect for her courage.

Then Fleming and Moriarty appeared. The Irishman shook his head wonderingly when he grabbed Phil's hand. "The luck that ye have, Phil Ward! How ye learned where Pennard was, I'll never know, and why they had not divided the payroll is another miracle. But they had not, and me and Fleming found it."

"The men are being paid right now," Fleming nodded at Phil's unspoken question. "They think you're a hell of a fine guy and they've forgotten all about hanging you."

"Agren?" Miles asked, arising. Fleming shrugged.

"I don't know. He's disappeared. Probably going hell-bent for some place else."

"I hope not," Miles said. "I'd like to spend some time with him." He glared at Pennard. "But in the meantime you'll do. Come on! The

Territory's going to board and room you for a mighty long time, though I doubt if you'll enjoy Yuma Prison."

After Miles and his prisoner left, Fleming told Phil how he and Tim, with a couple of clerks from Tim's office, had found the payroll money buried deep in a sawdust pile.

"It was safe enough," Fleming said. "Who'd think of looking there for it? They would have shown a neat little profit on that little deal in the canyon."

He insisted that Phil stay in the office so that word would get around town that the men were being paid. Phil objected, but Fleming wanted to be sure. Tim went out finally and soon came back, beaming.

"What Christians a little money can make of black-hearted spalpeens! They're lined up far down the street and the envelopes are being handed them. Sure, and ye should hear the blessings they call on the head of Phil Ward."

Fleming laughed dryly. "Then I guess it's safe. You'll come to the house, Phil. You'll need rest and a decent supper."

Phil nodded. After bringing the payroll to Tim's office, Fleming had hurried home and found Carol there, worried and distraught. He had told her what had happened and then had raced back to his own office. Now he looked sharply at Phil.

"Carol will want to see you."

"And I want to see her," Phil said firmly. Fleming looked pleased but said nothing.

They left the office. Once again the street, gaudy with bunting, was a place of celebration, not violence and death. They had taken only a few steps when someone called and Phil whipped about. Three of his construction workers came up, laughing. They were a little drunk and slapped him on the back, insisting he have a drink with them.

Phil managed a smile and begged off. He and Fleming finally broke loose and turned into a deserted side street.

Now the engineer said things about Agren he had not been free to speak before. Carol had been taken by the man, but Fleming had never been sure, sensing a basic weakness in his character. Phil listened, saying little, thinking much. He could see the future clear and bright before him now. Reiger and Trego dead, Pennard on his way to jail—there was no more fear of ambush or rustling. Agren was also finished. Fleming would move quickly to find some contractor to take Agren's place and the railroad could now be built to the Colorado without interruption.

Nor could Agren again cast his shadow over the Flemings. If things worked out right, Phil could again establish himself in Carol's thoughts. Given time, it might progress into something even finer. Phil clamped down on those ideas, telling himself that chance was afar off.

They came into Fleming's street and approached the house. They were still some distance away when the front door flew open. Carol walked to the edge of the steps, stood poised. Phil's breath caught in his throat. What a beautiful girl! No wonder Agren wanted her.

She rushed down the steps and ran toward them, eager and welcoming. Phil's stride increased and he hardly heard Fleming's chuckle. Phil could see the happy smile on her lips, the shine in her eyes.

A slight movement in a tangle of bushes beyond the house caught his attention. Agren burst out, hair disarrayed, eyes wild. He held a gun and the weapon swept up. Phil's face blanched. Carol was directly between him and Agren.

He threw himself at the girl and roughly shoved her aside. He had a brief glimpse of her stunned expression, her sudden little cry of surprise and hurt. His hand dipped to his holster, clearing the Colt and leveling it. He fired quickly, and knew he had missed.

Agren flinched, his gun still leveled. Panic came into the handsome face and he threw a single wild shot at Phil and turned and ran. The bullet went wide. Phil jerked to a halt, leveled his own gun. He could easily bring the man down.

Agren ploughed to a halt as half a dozen men circled him. Phil recognized Miles and some of his deputies. There was a brief scuffle and then it was over.

Phil holstered his Colt. He gently helped Carol to her feet. She looked beyond him at the group that took Agren away. Her lips quivered and a mist came to her eyes. Phil understood and he looked up at Fleming as the engineer stepped close.

"Take her into the house, Ray. I'll be with you in a few minutes."

Fleming took Carol's arm and led her back to the house. Miles came up, grinning.

"That was a close one. We figured he might show here, thought he was maybe inside the house. I'd formed a ring to make sure we got him when you and Fleming came. Sure surprised us all when Agren popped out of the bushes."

"No one's hurt," Phil said.

"But it could've happened. Anyhow, it's the last ambush that jasper will ever make. Him and Pennard will be a fine pair of cellmates."

At last the sheriff walked away. Phil watched him go, feeling the last of his worries lift from his shoulders. He slowly turned and faced the Fleming house. It seemed to welcome him.

He knew that Carol must be inside, perhaps crying. Phil could understand. She had believed in someone and he had failed her. In time she would find a new balance and adjust. Then perhaps she would understand how Phil had felt all along.

Maybe—just maybe he could once more invite her out to the Flying W. Maybe he would be able to tell her that he had loved her from the first moment he had seen her.

Hope flooded him and his shoulders squared. That's the way it would happen—maybe he'd tell her before the rails reached the Colorado.

It would be a fitting and wonderful end to a tremendous project. Phil walked to the house, his eyes alight.

Center Point Large Print
600 Brooks Road / PO Box 1
Thorndike ME 04986-0001 USA

(207) 568-3717

US & Canada:
1 800 929-9108
www.centerpointlargeprint.com